FORBIDDEN

FORBIDDEN

Kelley Armstrong

ILLUSTRATIONS BY LISSETH KAY

Subterranean Press 2012

First Edition

ISBN
978-1-59606-535-2

Subterranean Press
PO Box 190106
Burton, MI 48519

www.subterraneanpress.com

Morgan

MORGAN WALSH STRUGGLED to get the map open over the steering wheel, preferably without detouring into the ditch. It really wasn't a maneuver to be attempted by someone who hadn't driven in almost two years. When a horn blasted, he glanced up to see headlights in his lane. He cursed and yanked the wheel as the pickup roared past, kids shouting out rolled-down windows.

"Yeah, yeah," he muttered.

He shoved the map onto the passenger seat and peered out the windshield. There had to be a town along here somewhere. It was ninety miles to Syracuse, and he was starving. He *shouldn't* be starving. He'd spent the last two years in Alaska, living as a wolf, only eating every few days. Now he couldn't seem to go a few *hours* without his stomach threatening to devour itself.

He glanced at the side of the road. He should just pull over and check the map, but the shoulder was slick with snow. Snow. In early November. Even Anchorage didn't see this much of the white stuff so soon.

As he thought that, more began to fall. He flicked on the wipers and remembered his brother's voice, from their call, three days ago.

"Got a foot of snow last week. If you're coming home, you should do it soon. You know how it can get."

Oh, yeah. Morgan knew. Compared to winter in Newfoundland, Alaska was positively balmy.

"You *are* coming home, right?"

"Maybe for Christmas."

They both knew it was a lie. Morgan had gotten out; he wasn't going back. It wasn't the shitty weather that kept him away. Even in the breathtaking wilds of Alaska, he'd dreamed of rocky coasts and pounding surf. He'd even dreamed of winds that could knock the breath from your lungs and set your eyes blazing.

But he hadn't dreamed of life there, with his father and his brother, up before dawn, fishing for cod stocks that'd been depleted twenty years ago by factory fishing. And he hadn't dreamed of long nights in their cabin, far from any semblance of civilization, listening to his father rage against the DFO—and rage against Morgan, too, when he'd suggest it might be time to find a new livelihood. Walshes were fishermen and, by God, that's what they'd keep doing until it killed them.

Morgan had decided it was, all things considered, not really the way he cared to die. Or to live. So, at twenty-four, he'd packed a bag and set out to see what else the world had to offer. Four years later, he was still looking.

He hadn't told his brother where he was going now. If he even said the words "New York State," Blaine would have flipped out. Might even have come after his little brother. Which wasn't such a bad idea—it might be the only way to get Blaine off the Rock.

To the Walshes, as to most North American werewolves, New York meant one thing—the home of the American Pack. Growing up, Morgan had heard stories of the Pack the way other kids heard stories of the bogeyman and guys in white vans. The Pack. Madmen and murderers, every last one of them, endlessly scouring the country for innocent, peace-loving werewolves and slaughtering them for sport. *Stay in Newfoundland*, his dad said, *or the Pack will find you.*

Nearly eighteen months ago, the Pack did find him. They'd been in Alaska hunting other werewolves. Not for sport, but because the others were exactly the kind of wolves his father claimed the Pack were. Madmen and murderers. Rapists and man-eaters.

The Pack had invited Morgan to visit when he was done with his wolf experiment. They wanted to recruit him. They hadn't said that exactly, but he'd gotten the hint—come and hang out with us, and if we think you're a decent sort, we'd like to sign you up.

Was that what Morgan wanted? He had no idea. But it couldn't hurt to stop by. Just passing through, remembered they were there, decided to call and say hi, maybe take them out to dinner.

Speaking of dinner... His stomach rumbled again. In the distance, he could see what looked like a town sign. He peered through the falling snow until it came into view. Then he blinked. And laughed.

It was indeed a town sign...with a snarling wolfman welcoming visitors to Westwood, home of the champion Westwood Werewolves. Across the bottom, the sign declared "Westwood Loves Its Werewolves!"

Morgan chuckled to himself. "Oh, that's just too good to pass up."

MORGAN FOUND A diner at the end of the main street. There were only two cars in the lot, both covered in snow, but the light seeping through the windows gave him hope.

It was open. Empty, though. Through the window he could see a server reading a book. As he walked in, he noticed the sign on the window: 10% off for all Werewolves and their families.

Wonder if they'll give me the discount.

HE DIDN'T ASK for the discount, even jokingly. When you live in a world where werewolves exist only in books and movies, it's usually safer to keep it that way.

So no discount. He did get good food, though. He guessed you'd call it home-cooking, but it wasn't the kind of fare he ever got at home. His dad was a meat-and-potatoes man. Heavy on the potatoes, usually, unless he'd been lucky enough to hunt up deer or rabbit, sometimes even a moose. Tonight's dinner *was* meat-and-potatoes—meatloaf with scalloped potatoes—but it was a damned sight better than anything his father ever cooked. And the apple pie was definitely off their home menu. Morgan was finishing his second slice when the server stopped by.

"Hungry, I see," she said.

He flashed her a big smile. "Always."

She returned the smile and gave him a good view of her cleavage as she cleared his dishes. She hadn't shown much interest in her novel since he'd arrived. He got the message: there was more than food on the menu tonight, at least for him.

She was cute, in a dyed-blond, being-Homecoming-queen-was-the-best-day-of-my-life way. Comfort food, like dinner. He was seriously tempted to partake. A hunger for food wasn't the only appetite that'd slammed back as he returned to human life. This one was less surprising—there hadn't been much opportunity for sex as a wolf. Sure, one of the females had thought he looked mighty fine, but *that* experience had definitely not been part of his experiment.

So he was making up for lost time, and he'd have been happy to let the cute server help, but he really did need to hit the road. Being in New York State meant he was technically trespassing on Pack territory. He couldn't afford to linger.

"Anything else I can get for you?" she asked, standing close enough for him to smell her rich, soapy scent.

"Just the check," he said with regret. "I need to hit the road before this snow—"

A wave of nausea rocked him. The room seemed to swirl, lights dimming. He gripped the edge of the table and blinked hard.

"You okay?" the server asked.

"Yeah." He took a deep breath and straightened.

"Maybe that second slice wasn't such a good idea?"

As he nodded, his back started to itch. He looked down at his hands. The skin bubbled, like something was trapped under it. He yanked his hands under the table, one rubbing the other.

Damn it. He needed to be more careful. Take things slower. Like *not* going on a cross-country trip when he was accustomed to being in wolf form.

He reached for his wallet and slapped a twenty on the table, then rose, hands shoved in his pockets.

"You sure you're okay?" the server asked. "You shouldn't be driving if you're not."

"I'm fine." His voice came out a little too close to a growl, vocal cords straining, and he coughed to cover it. "I'll walk it off first. Get some fresh air."

"We've got a couch in the back." She slid in front of him and smiled up. "Or my place is just down the road. I make a pretty good nurse. Got two terms of schooling before I dropped out."

He shook his head and started to walk away. She caught his sleeve. He wheeled, eyes blazing, fever coming fast.

"No," he said, his voice a deep growl.

She staggered back. He hurried out the door.

MORGAN TRAMPED THROUGH the snow, almost to his knees. Luckily, the diner, being on the edge of town, backed onto forest. He'd headed straight there, cursing himself the whole way.

He should have Changed last night. He should Change *every* night until his body got used to being human. Sure, twice a week had been fine until now. Sure, willingly transforming nightly was akin to volunteering for nightly anesthesia-free surgery. But he could not take chances. Seeing the look on that server's face, he knew he'd taken a chance. And on Pack territory, too.

Goddamn it!

The snowfall lightened as he trudged deeper into the forest, but he barely noticed, too caught up in his thoughts. What exactly had the server seen? Did his face start Changing? Or was she only startled because he'd growled at her? He hoped that was it. God, he hoped that was it.

A branch slapped his face and he shoved it aside, growling, only to smack into a tree trunk. He blinked and rubbed his eyes. Everything looked slightly out of focus. He blinked harder.

He felt disoriented, like he had in the diner. That wasn't normally part of the Change. How long had he been driving? He calculated. Shit. Too long. No sleep. No exercise. Not nearly enough caffeine. That might explain this sudden need to Change.

He stumbled into the nearest clearing. Off came the clothing, shivers turning to near convulsions as he tried to hang it in branches, up off the snow.

Then he got down on all fours and started the transformation.

❧

THE PROCESS WENT faster than usual. No less painful, but the compressed timeframe made it seem better.

Lies we tell ourselves.

At least it was warmer with the wolf coat. His fur was dark red, like his hair. Once, when he'd been spotted by hunters in Alaska, they'd mistaken him for an Irish setter, which was kind of insulting. Maybe the coloring was close, but he was clearly a wolf. A wolf that weighed in at about a hundred and eighty pounds—his human weight—which made him nearly twice the size of a regular one. Still, being mistaken for a setter was better than having the hunters go back to town with stories of a massive, dark-red, green-eyed wolf.

He chuffed and looked around. Normally, it would be time to run. Work off the excess energy that came with being part canine. But he was woozy and dinner felt like a dead weight in his gut. A nice, leisurely evening stroll seemed more his speed—

"Are those footprints?" a distant voice said.

"Looks like it," a second man answered.

Shit. Rule One of Changing in a populated area? Get away from the damned population first.

Morgan had barely leapt from the clearing before he stumbled and plowed into a drift. He pushed up, shaking snow from his fur and looked back at the branch that had tripped him.

Where'd that come from?

He blinked and when he looked again, he saw two branches, blurred.

Where did they both *come from?*

Shit. He was really out of it. He should get farther into the forest and rest until it passed.

A branch cracked to his left. He peered through the trees. He could make out a bulky shadow about twenty feet away. Hunter? Bear? He wasn't in any condition to deal with either.

He ran. The snow had stopped falling, leaving the forest pitch-black, the dense treetops barely allowing any light from the quarter moon. His night vision had kicked in, but everything was blurred.

He stumbled over another branch and pitched head-first into a gully, his skull cracking against a half-buried boulder as he fell. When he hit bottom, he managed to get to his feet. He teetered a few steps, then dropped as everything went dark.

MORGAN SURFACED TO consciousness to the sound of a woman's voice. He groaned and struggled to remember the night before. Something about a woman. A server in a diner?

"Come on. Wake up!"

Obviously she was in a damned hurry to get him out the door. Was she married? Shit. He was usually careful about stuff like that.

It took some effort to pry open his eyes, and when he did, a blast of light almost made them close again. He squinted and saw a blurred figure bending over him. Then an icy wind blasted over his bare skin.

"Jesus," he muttered. "Someone close the damned—"

The figure above him came into focus. It was a very pretty dark-haired, dark-eyed woman, his age or a little older. Huh. He'd lucked out last night. Now if he could actually remember—

"Get up!" she said.

He blinked and rose on his elbows. Damn, it was cold. Why was it so—?

He got a good look at the woman. She wore a dark-brown parka over a khaki shirt and trousers. It was some kind of uniform. Including a gun in her hand. Pointed at him.

A ray of sunlight glinted off a police badge on her parka.

Morgan sat up fast, realizing as he did that he wasn't in a bed. He was lying in the snow. Naked. Surrounded by cops.

"Uh..." he began, as he looked around.

His gaze fell on the tracks in the snow. Wolf tracks.

Shit.

Jessica

WESTWOOD POLICE CHIEF Jessica Dales stood inside the station house door, struggling to close it against a gust of wind. She finally won the battle and paused to stamp the snow from her boots before she walked in. A blast of furnace-hot air greeted her. She closed her eyes and let her cheeks thaw before she stepped into the office.

Wes Kent looked up from his paperwork at the front desk.

"Weatherman's right," Jess said. "Another storm's blowing up. Crazy weather." She swiped snow from her hair, then hooked her thumb at the holding cell, just past an open doorway. "Speaking of crazy, is our streaker talking yet?"

"Nope," Kent said. "No ID either. I ran the plates. Seems he bought the car in Vancouver for a grand last week. Guy let him 'borrow' the plates for a few hundred more."

"Nice of him."

Jess walked to the open doorway and looked into the cell. Their new prisoner—their *only* prisoner—sat with his back to the bars. Before they'd located the car, they'd found his clothing in a nearby tree. It'd been soaking wet. They'd offered him a dry shirt and pants from some extras they kept in back, but he'd refused, putting on the wet ones instead.

"If he bought the car in Vancouver, he crossed the border," she said. "So he must have a passport."

"Should. By that accent, I'm guessing he's Scottish."

It was an odd accent, not one she remembered hearing before. She supposed it could be Scottish, but that seemed a strange fit for a guy who looked like he had a generous dose of Native American blood, despite the reddish hair and green eyes.

"I'll head back out and search his car," she said. "We know where he started his trip. If we can figure out where he was going, that will help. A place. A name. Anything."

"How about both?" Kent asked. "Plus a phone number."

He held out a map with a thick black circle around Syracuse, New York. Beside it, someone had written "Elena" and a phone number.

Jess took out her cell. ~

One

I STOOD JUST BEYOND the study doorway, out of sight. The low-burning fireplace tried to lure me in, with its inviting crackle and pop, rich smoky smell and tendrils of heat. Clay's low voice was an enticement, too. After three days of snowstorms, I just wanted to curl up on the sofa with him, drowse in the firelight and—

"You already moved!"

"I didn't take my fingers off it!"

"That still counts. Dad! Tell her it counts!"

Three days of snowstorms. One sprained ankle. Two serious cases of cabin fever.

"Let's go outside, guys," Clay said. "I'll pull Kate on the toboggan."

Make that three cases.

I steeled myself and walked through the doorway. Clay was on the couch, leaning over as they played chess on the floor. Logan and Kate had just turned five in September. With every birthday, there's a part of me that hopes this is the one where their energy levels will drop a little. I might as well hope that the moon will turn purple. They're the children of werewolves—those energy levels aren't dropping until they're a *hundred*-and-five.

"I don't wanna get pulled," Kate said. "I wanna walk!"

"You can't," Logan said. "You sprained your ankle, stupid."

Kate jumped on her brother. "I'm not stupid!"

Clay grabbed Kate's sweater and lifted her off her brother, snarling and spitting, more wildcat than wolf.

"Logan," I said as I walked in. "Did you forget the rule? Call her stupid and you earn an hour in your room."

He looked up at me. "That's not the rule. The rule is an hour if we call each other an *idiot*."

"Logan…"

He scowled. "It's her fault we can't go outside. She's the one who fell."

"Because you pushed me off the slide," Kate said.

Logan leaped up. "I did not! You fell and I grabbed your coat. I was trying to *help* you." He spun on me. "I wouldn't push her. Tell her, Momma."

"I know. She does, too. She's just angry."

I scooped him up, ignoring his wriggling, and sat on Jeremy's recliner with him on my lap. I looked over at Clay, holding an equally squirming Kate.

"I'll grab the duct tape if you find the rope," I said.

He chuckled.

"I heard that," Logan grumbled.

I kissed his cheek and got a scowl in return. We sat there for a minute, just holding the kids. Cuddling and calming them. Or restraining them. It's a fine line some days.

I looked at Kate, her blond curls swinging as she struggled to get free. Above her, Clay bent down, whispering. There was no mistaking them for anything but father and daughter, with matching blue eyes and golden curls, Kate's down past her shoulders, Clay's cropped close. Similar in temperament as well as looks. Jeremy says that Clay was more like Logan as a child, quiet and serious, but Kate definitely takes after him now, squirming and shooting furious glances his way, refusing to settle until she damned well wanted to settle.

Logan had already calmed down. He was still angry, saving his energy for the glares he kept firing at his sister. He has my dark-blue eyes and my straight hair, though his is a deeper shade than my silver-blond. I'd like to think his off-the-charts IQ comes from his Mom, but I have to cede that to his PhD father. As for his uncanny ability to maintain long, angry silences, I have no idea where that comes from. Really.

"Okay," I said. "We need a plan. How about some apart-time? Dad will take Logan for a walk while—"

"That's not fair!" Kate said. "I want to go for a walk, too!"

"I was going to suggest you help me bake cookies."

"But I want to bake cookies!" Logan said. "And we haven't finished our chess game. You can't let her quit just because I was winning—"

"You weren't winning," Kate said. "I had a plan."

Her brother snorted.

Kate's eyes blazed. "I did. You'll see."

She jumped back onto the floor. Logan scrambled down beside her.

The phone rang. Clay and I collided pouncing on it. I won, grabbing the receiver and jogging away. Yes, it's a sad day when getting the phone is a victory. Especially in a household where it normally rings through to voice mail, with three people sitting within reach of a receiver.

"Is this Elena?" said a woman's voice when I answered.

"Yes…"

"This is Jess Dales, chief of police for Westwood, New York. I have someone here…"

I listened as she explained. When I hung up, Clay said, "Trouble?"

"Maybe. I need to talk to Jeremy."

CLAY SHUTTLED THE kids to the kitchen and left them there to make sandwiches while he followed me to Jeremy's studio.

"Do you think that's such a good idea?" I nodded toward the kitchen. "There are knives."

"I don't think the situation has reached that point." He glanced back. "The really sharp ones are locked up, though, right?"

"They are. It'd be minor injuries. More likely a jam-flinging fight."

"After which we can make them take turns having baths and cleaning the kitchen, which means at least twenty minutes of apart-time." Another glance over his shoulder. "Should I go back and get out the honey, too?"

"Tempting."

The door to Jeremy's studio was closed. Well, not exactly—he'd left it open a few inches, but for Jeremy that was a clear "do not disturb" sign. And one even the kids would respect. I rapped first.

"Come in."

Jeremy was standing at his easel, with his back to us. His shirt sleeves were pushed up, feet bare, socks lying on a nearby chair. We'd gone for a walk outside earlier talking about Alpha business. When we'd come in, I'd grabbed him a dry pair, but obviously he'd gotten too wrapped up in his painting to put them on. Just like he'd gotten too wrapped up to realize he really shouldn't run his hands through his hair when they were dappled with paint. There were blue streaks through his silver-threaded dark hair. Maybe I'd tell him about them; maybe I wouldn't.

I couldn't see what he was working on, and I didn't try to peek. He'd show it when it was ready. For now, he just lifted a finger and finished his brushstroke. Then he pulled out his earbuds. Jeremy never paints to music. Another sign that the chaos around here had become a little too much even for our unflappable Alpha.

"Remember Morgan Walsh?" I said as I perched on the window seat. "Newfoundland werewolf in Alaska?"

"The mutt who was living as a wolf?" Clay said. "Kinda hard to forget."

True. It wasn't something that happened very often. So rarely, in fact, that we'd added a page for Morgan to the Legacy—our book of Pack and werewolf history. There was a section for oddities. He fit right in. While his "experiment" was unusual, the guy himself had seemed normal enough. Until this call came.

"He was *what?*" Clay said when I finished explaining. "On Pack *territory*? Did I say the guy was a little crazy, darling?"

"He's not crazy. Just young. Trying to find himself. Some guys go backpacking in the Himalayas. He tried living as a wolf."

Clay's snort said "a little crazy" still described it. This from a guy who was himself more wolf than human. Yet as much as he loved being in wolf-form, it wasn't anything he'd choose long-term. I wouldn't either, but I could better understand Morgan's identity crisis. Clay has always known exactly what he was. It took me a lot longer to figure it out. Some days I'm still trying.

"We can overlook the trespassing," I said. "It seems he was heading to see us."

"And the rest of it?" Clay said. "Being found by the cops? Naked? In the snow? Surrounded by paw prints?"

"That might require intervention."

"You think?"

I shot him a glare, then looked back at Jeremy, who'd been quietly listening. "We could ignore this. Let Morgan dig himself out of the mess. But considering it's on Pack territory…"

"We should handle it," Jeremy said. "If he had your phone number he was planning to announce his visit. That means his detour was a youthful indiscretion, not a deliberate act."

"A big indiscretion," Clay grumbled. "The guy's older than Reese. That's not *youthful* enough to excuse it."

"How old is he again?" Jeremy asked me. "Twenty-seven, twenty-eight?"

"Yeah, about that."

Jeremy took off his music player and wrapped the earbud cord around it. "I seem to recall that's young enough to do something rash and impulsive. Something that might have far-reaching consequences."

Jeremy's voice was low, his tone casual, but his words still made Clay flinch. Clay had been that age himself when he bit me.

"I'll drive up and take care of it," Jeremy said.

Clay and I both stared at him.

"Yes?" he said, pocketing his player.

"You're the Alpha," I said. "You make decisions and send out your trusty minions to enforce them. That would be us."

Kate shrieked from the kitchen. "Give that back!"

"I believe I should handle this," Jeremy said. "You've been preparing to take over as Alpha. Likewise, I should prepare to resume duties as a Pack member."

"Nice try," I said. "No adventures while you're still Alpha. That's the rule."

Clay clapped him on the back as we headed out. "Don't worry. We'll take care of this."

"It's not a matter that requires both—" Jeremy began.

Logan raced past the open doorway, a sandwich in each hand. Kate stumped after him, bound foot pounding the floor.

"The Alpha-elect needs a bodyguard," Clay said. "That's another rule. Sorry. Love to stay. Gotta go."

We slipped out after the kids passed. We snuck to the front door and grabbed our coats and boots. Jeremy followed.

"Enjoy it while you can," he said to me. "Once you're Alpha, no more adventures."

"Pfft. That's *your* rule. When I'm Alpha, I'm changing it. That's the beauty of being the bitch in charge."

Clay grinned and handed me my gloves. At the sound of footsteps, Jeremy stepped into the foyer with us. We all stood silently watching as Kate clomped past. She had both sandwiches mashed in one hand and was taking a bite. When she didn't notice us, I exhaled in relief and grabbed the door handle.

"Mom!" Logan shouted.

"We'll be back before bedtime," I whispered to Jeremy.

"You'd better be," he said as we made our escape.

Two

STONEHAVEN IS A rural estate outside the small town of Bear Valley, New York. The closest city is Syracuse. According to the GPS in Jeremy's SUV, Westwood was almost an hour west of that, off a regional highway. We'd been driving for about thirty minutes when the snow started falling again and the radio announcer declared another blizzard was set to hit before nightfall.

"I don't like the sounds of that," I said.

"It'll be fine." Clay turned up the windshield wipers. "I'm planning on getting this done before dinner. And since we didn't say we'd be back until bedtime, that gives us a few extra hours."

"For a nice meal, without screaming kids and flying food?"

"I was thinking more like..." He pointed to a roadside motel as we passed. "Unless you'd rather go out to dinner."

I grinned. "Not unless we're done early enough to swing into Syracuse and get a hotel with room service."

He put his foot on the gas.

❧

We finally reached Westwood...complete with a werewolf leaping off the town welcome sign.

"Walsh chose to Change *here*?" Clay said as we passed the sign.

"There must be a good explanation."

Clay jerked his chin toward an old feed mill on the edge of town. Through the snow, I could make out a wall mural of a snarling werewolf.

"Yeah, there's an explanation, all right," Clay said. "The guy's an idiot."

I refrained from comment. Whatever Morgan's excuse, it had better be a good one. By this stage, I was starting to think Clay had a point. Which meant Morgan Walsh's bad day was about to get a whole lot worse.

❧

We parked on the main street, a few doors down from the police station. As we tramped along the snowy sidewalk, we passed a shop with a huge "Warning: Werewolf Territory" sign in the window.

"Did I mention the idiot part?" he said.

I sighed.

"If I were in charge, I'd let this mutt hang himself."

"Which is why you're not going to be in charge."

"And damned glad of it," he said. "I don't care how good his excuse is—"

I spun to ward off…Nothing. There was nothing and it took a moment for me to even process why I was standing there, fists starting to rise. I hadn't heard anything. It was just…a feeling. The hair on the back of my neck rising, some deep-rooted instinct flicking on my fight-or-flight response.

"Elena?" Clay said.

Down the street, someone was coming out of a shop. On the road, a single car was trying to get traction, engine whining. That was it. Just one car and one person.

"Sorry," I said, shaking it off. "That's what happens when I don't leave the house in a week. I get outside and I feel like someone's watching."

"Small towns. Someone's always watching."

"No kidding." I took a deep breath. "All right then. Let's sort this mess out and go home."

THE POLICE STATION was actually just a storefront along the main street, wedged between the hardware store and the bank. I was a little concerned about signs in the hardware store advertising bolt-cutters and shotguns. Maybe the Westwood cops were bored, hoping to convince some drunken local that breaking into the bank next door was easier than he thought.

The station's front door opened into a small foyer. A sign asked visitors to leave their boots on the mat. Clay ignored it. I was pulling mine off when I saw the puddles leading inside, suggesting no one else had obeyed either. So I left mine on, though I did feel guilty about it. I'd spent most of my life doing as I was told; it's a hard habit to break.

There were only two officers in the main room, neither of them working very hard. One was a man in his early fifties, sitting behind the desk, talking to the other officer—a young woman sipping what I presumed was coffee until my nose told me it was hot cocoa.

When we entered, both officers looked over.

"Elena Michaels," I said, walking over, hand extended. "Chief Dales called me?"

"I did," the young woman said, stepping forward to shake my hand. That threw me for a moment. In a small town, I'd been surprised the police chief was a woman; I certainly didn't expect one who didn't look past her thirtieth birthday.

A noise came through an open doorway. I looked to see Morgan gripping the bars of a cell.

"Elena? Um, hey. What are you...?" His gaze traveled over my shoulder, where Clay stood. "Uh, Clayton..."

Clay walked toward the cell. Morgan took a slow step back, suddenly looking very grateful for those metal bars.

"Er, I can explain," Morgan said.

"You'd better hope so," Clay said, too low for the non-werewolves to pick up.

I turned back to Chief Dales. "I'm really sorry about this. We were worried sick when he didn't show up last night. I guess he made a pitstop for a few beers." I mustered a glare in Morgan's direction. "Good thing those coyotes didn't decide to take a taste of him."

"The paw prints were too big for coyotes," Chief Dales said. "And we didn't find any human tracks. Just the paw prints. All around him."

I sighed and looked at Morgan, shaking my head. "You were out there long enough for the snow to cover your footprints? You're lucky you didn't get frostbite anyplace you really don't want frostbite."

When I looked at the police chief, she caught my gaze and held it. I gazed back, calm and cool.

"Is that what you think happened?" she asked, after a ten-second stare-down.

"What else?"

"What else, indeed?"

More staring. Which I'm sure would have worked out a whole lot better for her if I was a small-town perp, not a werewolf who'd spent twenty years covering up mutt kills and, sometimes, dead mutts. I waited patiently until she spoke again.

"Do you want to hear my theory?" she asked.

"Sure."

She stepped back. She tried to make it casual, just moving, not retreating. But that's another thing about being a werewolf for so long—I've become almost as fluent in body language as I am in English, especially when it comes to expressions of dominance and submission.

"You've seen our town has an…affinity for werewolves," she said. "I think that has something to do with your boy's run through the forest."

I laughed and glanced at Morgan, who looked worried. "What? You got drunk and decided to go werewolf hunting?"

"Not hunting," Chief Dales said. "Staging. He's not the first person to try it. Frat boy passing through, decides to pull a prank on the local yokels."

"Frat boy?" Morgan said. "How young do you think I am?"

Clay moved in front of Morgan. I couldn't see the look he gave, but it shut Morgan down fast.

"Not young enough for this crap," I called to him, then turned to Chief Dales. "I'm so sorry. He's a friend of the family. We haven't seen him in years. Obviously, he has a few issues" —a glare in Morgan's direction—"to work through. If there's anything we can do to fix this…"

She walked back behind the desk with the older officer, who'd been watching in silence. "It's his lucky day. Got another storm coming in. Otherwise, I'd slap a public indecency charge on his ass. I expect him to present his ID so I can file a report, but otherwise, just get him out of my sight. And out of Westwood."

Jessica

JESS LED HER three guests out of the station. Then she stood at the door and watched them leave. Once they were out of sight, she exhaled, and leaned against the wall.

A close call. Damned close.

She should have made the connection. Guy turns up in their woods surrounded by paw prints, with a map marked with Syracuse and the name Elena. As in Elena Michaels, the only female werewolf in the supernatural universe.

Years ago, when Jess was at college in Buffalo, she'd made contact with a few local supernaturals. That always helped, for support and companionship. When she told them she'd gotten a job with the Westwood police, one guy had said, "Isn't that werewolf territory?" She'd thought he meant the local football team. He hadn't.

"The werewolf Pack lives up there," he said. "Somewhere near Syracuse."

Someone else said they'd heard the rumor, but it was just that—a rumor. The Pack lived on the west coast, one claimed. Another said there *was* no Pack—werewolves weren't bright enough to organize like that. They were just dumb brutes running around slaughtering people. Like in the movies.

Jess did her research anyway. She wasn't taking a job as a cop in werewolf territory. But how exactly *did* you research that? Google "werewolves in New York State?" That was a ticket straight to Weirdsville. She'd searched police files instead, looking for signs of possible werewolf kills. Nothing.

So she'd chalked it up to rumor. Yet, having heard it, she couldn't help paying attention when other supernaturals talked about werewolves. She'd eventually learned there definitely was a Pack. One member was a woman named Elena Michaels. It was a common enough name and, really, not worth researching—she didn't have time for idle curiosity. She'd heard other names over the years, including Elena's mate, a guy named Clayton who was supposed to be a really nasty son-of-a-bitch. But none of those stories ever mentioned Syracuse or upstate New York, so they didn't concern her.

Until now.

Even when the woman had introduced herself, the light bulb hadn't flashed. Racial stereotyping, she supposed.

Jess didn't think she was one of those who believed werewolves were all Neanderthal brutes, but apparently she did have some preconceptions. And they didn't cover a friendly blonde who, with her ponytail and worn blue jeans, looked like a movie star going incognito. It definitely didn't cover the guy with her, a seriously hot thirty-something who wouldn't look out of place on a billboard—preferably wearing as little as possible.

When Walsh called him Clayton, Jess had nearly choked on her cocoa. Even then, there was a moment when she told herself she had to be mistaken. Right up until she saw Walsh shrinking back as the guy bore down on him.

There were werewolves in Westwood. Three of them. Real werewolves. It would be damned funny if it didn't scare the shit out of her.

Jess took another deep breath.

No reason to overreact. It was a freak encounter. Walsh must have been driving past, seen the signs and been unable to resist a detour. He'd stopped at the diner and had a few shots. More than a few, according to the server, Marnie. The booze had washed away his common sense, and he'd extended his visit to include a run in their forest.

Now the Pack had come and scooped him up. From the looks of things, he was in serious shit. They'd completely bought her "theory," meaning they had no reason to stick around. They'd bustle Walsh out of town and steer clear for a very long time. Which suited her just fine.

Jess straightened and strode back into the station. ~

Three

WHEN JEREMY FIRST told me I was his choice for Alpha, I thought he'd lost it. Maybe it was stress. Maybe a fever. Clearly something, because the idea was ludicrous. Okay, I'll be honest for a moment and put aside the false humility. I didn't think, "I can't handle it." I could. Oh, I'd struggle. I'd screw up. I'd never really replace Jeremy. But I *could* be Alpha. That didn't mean it wasn't crazy.

First, I'm not a hereditary werewolf, obviously. The gene passes through the male line. I didn't grow up in the Pack either. Even after Clay bit me, I spent ten years boomeranging between the Pack and my old dream of a "normal" life. Eventually I came to realize that Pack life *was* normal for me. Everything I'd wanted—stability, family, acceptance—I found there.

But that still means I've only really embraced werewolf life for a decade. Plus there's the gender issue. The werewolf world is truly a male-dominated society, mostly because there aren't any other women in it. With the Pack, I think that actually worked in my favor—they didn't quite know what to expect, so they didn't really expect anything. I could be myself.

Beyond our territory, though, I can win a dozen challenge fights, and I won't be accepted as "one of the guys." I'm a chick in wolf's clothing. That makes me mate material. It also makes me revenge material, for all the mutts who'd love to hurt Clay. But it does not make me a "real" werewolf, much less an Alpha.

I'd come to realize, though, that Jeremy didn't have a lot of choice for successors. Clay wouldn't take the job and, let's be honest, I don't think Jeremy would give it to him anyway. There was nobody more important to Jeremy than his foster son, but there was also nobody he understood better. If Clay became Alpha, all the reforms Jeremy had instituted would begin a slow backward slide. Clay would try to respect them, but he didn't always understand the rationale behind them.

As for the rest of the Pack, no one else was suited to the post either. Antonio was a year older than Jeremy. Nick was... not Alpha material. Nor was Karl Marsten. Maybe someday Reese and Noah would be, but one was in college and the other in high school. That left yours truly. Which meant that, when faced with a problem like Morgan Walsh, I could no longer just call up Jeremy and say, "Hey, what do you want me to do?" I was expected to make my own decisions. Which, sometimes, really sucked.

But the problem was mostly resolved. Morgan had "found" his ID and Chief Dales had processed his official release. We were leaving Westwood.

Snow was still falling, coming down a little heavier, which put some extra speed in our strides. It was mid-afternoon. There was definitely time for a stop in Syracuse. Which should not, admittedly, be my first priority. But I wasn't Alpha yet, I was allowed the occasional spurt of bad judgement. I needed to decide what to do with Morgan in the meantime, but that was best done after we'd hightailed it out of Westwood.

Morgan hadn't said a word since we'd left the station. None of us had. We were just walking, with Clay on one side of me and Morgan on the other, as far from Clay as he could get.

"Look, I know I screwed up," Morgan said finally.

"You think?" Clay muttered.

"But I did *not* ask them to call Elena. I would never have gotten you guys involved."

"Which was the last in your long string of mistakes," I said. "If you get in trouble like that, you call us. Otherwise, if the problem gets out of hand, you don't get me coming to your rescue. You just get him." I nodded toward Clay.

Morgan tried for a smile. "Complete with chainsaw?"

"Nah," Clay said. "You risk exposing us? On our territory? You don't get the chainsaw. I hang you from the nearest tree, rip you open and let the vultures feast."

"Er, I can explain."

I stopped beside Jeremy's SUV and opened the back door. "We'll get to that part. But not here. We're going to take you to your car. Then I'll drive it, following you and Clay, to someplace where we can chat. Far from here."

We all climbed in. I kept one eye on Morgan, in case he decided to bolt, but he just fastened his seat belt. Clay started the SUV and put it in drive. It lurched forward with an odd thump. He frowned and pressed the gas. Another lurch. Another bump.

"Shit," Clay muttered.

He threw it into park and got out. I did the same and looked down at the front passenger-side tire.

"Flat tire," I called over the hood. "Good thing we have a spare."

"Yeah, but we don't have two."

"Seriously?"

I walked to the front of the SUV. Both tires were flat. Not much chance that was accidental. I peered along the snowy road, but we were the only people in sight.

"Guess we're taking your car," I said to Morgan as he climbed out. "We'll call a truck for this. It's a long tow, but I don't want to stick around."

❧

WE MADE THE trek down the main street to the diner, where Morgan had left his car. As we walked, he explained the events of the night before.

"And that's how they found me." He took a deep breath. "I screwed up. No alcohol involved—I know better than that. And I wouldn't have Changed so close to town if I thought I was in any shape to drive out. But obviously I'm not accustomed to being in human form yet and I let myself get too tired. Add in a big meal and something just...went wonky. In my defense, I can say that it's never happened before. I've been Changing every three days since I left Alaska, and that's worked out just fine. But, yes, I screwed up. I know that. I'll—"

He stopped. "Son of a bitch!"

Morgan broke into a run. I squinted through the falling snow to see a single car in the diner parking lot. Morgan's car, I presumed. Someone in a parka was crouched beside it, slashing the rear tire.

"What the hell?" Clay muttered.

He took off after Morgan. I followed.

"Hey!" Morgan shouted when we drew close.

The vandal looked up. He was dressed in a dark parka, the hood tunneled, hiding his face. Seeing us, he took off running toward the forest.

I raced to the car and crouched beside it. The rear passenger tire was slashed. When I ducked to look underneath, I saw the same on the other side.

"Damn it!" I said. "Two tires here, too. We'll need to—"

I straightened and looked around the parking lot. I was talking to myself. The guys were gone.

Four

IT WAS A scene straight from a horror movie. The heroic—and slightly brain-dead—guys go racing into the forest after the madman with the knife. The clueless blonde stumbles after them, yelling, "Guys! Hey, guys! Wait up!"

If it was a horror movie, I'd be about two cinematic minutes from meeting a grisly end as I realized—too late—that the deranged killer had purposely led my menfolk into the woods to separate me from them. Also, I'd be topless.

As it was, I was tramping through knee-deep snow in a very unsexy pair of hiking boots and a decade-old ski-jacket. I was also wearing sock monkey mittens—a gift from Kate last year. It's a new kind of horror movie. Forget screaming, half-naked co-eds. Time to slaughter a few "did I even put on makeup before I left the house?" moms.

"Couldn't just let it go, could you, guys?" I muttered as snow melted down the back of my neck. "Oh, no. Gotta catch the bastard. Can't let him get away with that." I snorted. "Men. You don't see me tearing off into a strange forest in the middle of a snow—"

I looked around. "Never mind."

I crouched and peered down at the snow-covered ground. I could smell the guys' scents, but their footprints were already covered as the snow came down hard.

I stood. "Clay! Morgan!"

No answer. Damn them. I should just go back to the car and wait. That would be the non-dumb-blonde thing to do. It would also be the non-Alpha-elect thing to do. I sighed. At least I was pretty sure knife-wielding guy was a vandal, not a serial killer. Even if he was, this blonde came with super-strength and a kick-ass secret disguise.

I continued along, following Clay's scent. Soon I could only see a few feet ahead of me.

Snow blind.

Damn it, guys. Five more minutes and I am *turning back—before I can't find my way out.*

I walked, mittens off, hands out, making sure I didn't waltz into a knife. Or, more likely, a tree. I did narrowly avoid a white birch that blended with the snow. As I touched it, my fingers ran across deep grooves in the bark. I moved closer for a better look.

There was a symbol carved in the trunk. It didn't look like mere woodland graffiti. When I brushed the snow away, I could see someone had rubbed a deep red substance into the grooves. Not blood—I'd smell that. Meant to look like blood, though?

I turned around, the snow no longer driving into my face, giving me a clearer view of my surroundings. I was in a circle of white birch, all with that red mark carved onto them.

I took out my cell phone for a photograph. That was almost instinctive. It had nothing to do with being a werewolf and everything to do with being the wife of an anthropologist specializing in religion and ritual. I was mildly curious, and knew Clay might be able to satisfy that curiosity. So I took pictures.

As I was pulling my mittens back on, something moved, off to the side. When I looked, the forest seemed empty. But I'd seen something. I knew I had.

"Clay?" I called. "Morgan?"

Brush crackled to my left. A shadow loomed over me. I spun, fists up.

Morgan looked down at my hands.

"Nice mittens," he said.

"They hit just fine," I said. "Which you will discover if you ever sneak up on me again." I lowered my fists. "A little warning next time, please."

"Sorry." He walked over and brushed snow off a partly-covered symbol. "Huh. Weird."

"Not really. Many pagan practitioners conduct rituals in the forest. Perfectly harmless rituals. I've never seen these marks before. Clay might know what they are. I wouldn't suggest asking him, though, unless you're prepared for a twenty-minute teaching moment." I looked past him. "Speaking of which, he's not with you?"

He shook his head. "I lost him a while ago. I figured I should head back and find you."

At least the guy had good Pack instincts. Always a bonus in a potential recruit, but I had a feeling that his viability had dipped since last night's episode. At least, it would in Clay's eyes. I was more interested in young mutts who could be shaped into good Pack members, having given up on recruiting experienced ones who were already suitable.

"Let's head back to town." I stepped from the birch grove and stared out into the seemingly endless expanse of white forest. "If we can find it."

I took my mittens off again and pulled out my cell phone. I raised it to get a lock on the GPS.

"Gotta love modern technology," I said.

I led Morgan out of the grove.

"You know," he said. "You could probably use that handy gadget to find Clayton, too. By calling him."

"That only works with people who also embrace modern technology. Clayton—"

I stopped as a smell drifted past on the breeze. I lifted my face to sniff better.

"You smell him?" Morgan said. "Damn. You *are* good. I can't pick up a damned thing out…"

He trailed off. I was already on the move, walking fast through the evergreens, pushing branches out of my way as Morgan jogged to keep up.

"It's not Clay," I said. "Thankfully."

I followed the scent to a massive evergreen.

"Oh, wait," Morgan said. "Now I'm catching a scent. Is that…?"

I crouched and pushed aside the ground-level branches to see something sheltered and hidden at the very base of the tree. It was a corpse. A long-dead, frozen, decomposed corpse.

"Definitely not Clay," Morgan murmured.

I pushed back the branches to get a better look at the body. It looked as if it had been out here a while—not long enough to completely decompose, but a good ways along that route. Judging by the clothing, it was a man. Fully grown. That's about all I could guess. Except for one last thing—it didn't look as if he'd curled up under this tree and died. The pose was too awkward for that. Someone had shoved him in here post-mortem.

Morgan crouched beside me. "I didn't do it."

"I didn't think you did."

"Thank you."

"Body's too decomposed. You only got to town yesterday."

"I'm not a man-killer." Morgan sounded annoyed.

"Yeah?" said a voice behind us. "Well, I've never met a mutt who claimed otherwise."

Clay walked over.

"No offense," I murmured to Morgan. "We've learned to be skeptical."

"So, what've we got here?" Clay didn't wait for an answer, but crouched down and pushed back the branches. "Huh."

I hunkered beside him as he examined the body. No expression crossed his face. No revulsion. No pity either. There was a time when that bothered me, when it seemed a sign that there was something missing in Clay, something vital, something that made us human. There was. Because he wasn't human.

Clay could barely remember a life when he wasn't a werewolf. He lacked the ability to look at a stranger and see anything more than a potential source of aid or threat. That's how the wolf sees anyone who isn't in his pack—either they can help you or they can kill you, and it's probably the latter.

That doesn't make him "less than human." He's perfectly capable of forming relationships—stronger ones than most humans could imagine. And he has no interest in hurting anyone who doesn't threaten his Pack. It just means that he can look at a body like this and he won't see the tragedy of a life cut short. He just sees a potential problem that could affect us.

"Something's taken a few bites," he said, leaning close enough to the corpse that my own gorge rose. "Can't tell if it's a scavenger or a predator. Seems to be missing a hand, too."

"We can't poke around too much if we're going to report it. Which is the big question."

Clay nodded and moved back, letting the branches cover the body.

"Report it?" Morgan said. "Why? It's been there a while, obviously. No one's going to know we found it." He paused. "I mean, yes, reporting it would be the right thing to do. He has a family out there somewhere, wondering what happened to him, and maybe a killer who's gone free—"

"Not our concern," Clay said, standing.

"Unfortunately," I added. Because it *was* unfortunate and that's exactly what I thought every time I had to hide a body or leave one hidden. That somewhere out there, a family would never be able to bury their dead, would never be able to mourn properly. But it couldn't be our concern. Werewolves had to put their Pack first.

"If we could bury it, that would be best," I said. "But the ground's frozen solid."

"Why can't we just leave it?"

"Because we've been here," Clay said. "We've left a shit-load of tracks to a dead body. We were chasing someone who might be watching us as we stand over a corpse. And we left our names—our real names—at that police station."

"It might continue to go undiscovered," I said. "But we can't take that chance. If he's found today, they'll contact us. If he's found next month, they'll probably check their records and remember the naked guy in the woods. We didn't have anything to do with this, so it's safest to play it on the level. As if we were just regular citizens. I'll—"

A noise off to my left made me pause. I looked out. Nothing was there, but once again, I had the distinct feeling I was being watched. I took a few steps into the woods, lifting a finger for Clay and Morgan to wait.

I walked about twenty paces in the direction of the noise. While it was still mid-afternoon, I swore the sun was dropping, shrouding the forest in long shadows.

When I saw what looked like snow-dimpled footprints, I bent. I brushed the layer of snow off and inhaled.

As I did, I sensed someone walking up behind me. Even with the wind going the other way, I knew who it was.

"Do you know what this meant?" I asked, lifting my bare index finger.

"Yeah," Clay said. "Wait one minute. I waited two." He came closer. "Are those tracks?"

"Yes." I pushed to my feet. "Ours."

I walked to Clay. Morgan hovered a few steps back.

"I just felt like we were being watched again," I said. "I heard something, too. But there's no sign of a trail. No scents on the breeze either." I shook my head. "I think I've been house-bound too long. I'm turning into a paranoid hermit."

We walked back to where we'd left the body.

"Better get this over with," I said. "Can one of you stay with it? So we don't lose the spot?"

"I'll stay." Morgan gave me a look. "And I promise not to snack."

Morgan

MORGAN HUDDLED ON the leeward side of the evergreen, rubbing his hands together. Elena and Clay had left without even commenting on his man-eater crack, as if he'd been seriously reassuring them. He shook his head. They really didn't get it. To them, considering all "mutts" potential man-eaters seemed to be a simple case of caution. Like not leaving cash lying around the house when you had contractors over. But it wasn't like that at all. It was like presuming all men lusted after thirteen-year-old girls until they proved they didn't. Insulting on a deep moral and personal level.

Morgan shivered, hunched against the cold and shoved his bare hands under his armpits. Maybe he'd made a mistake, coming to see the Pack. They weren't werewolves in the way he was, or his father and brother were. The three of them had grown up isolated from the very culture of being werewolf. His father and brother viewed it as an affliction. A genetic condition that you learned to live with. Morgan didn't agree, which was why he'd lived among wolves, to get in touch with that side of his nature. But to the Pack, being a werewolf wasn't just about being partly wolf. It really was an all-encompassing way of life.

Still, that did have an appeal, which was why he'd come. He'd found something in that Alaskan wolf pack that he'd never experienced before. A sense of community. He wasn't ever going to get that back home, where it was just the three of them, mingling with the outside world as little as possible.

Of course, the problem with the wolf pack was, well, they were wolves. Intellectually, it was a little stifling. So, from that perspective, the werewolf Pack seemed intriguing. Community and brotherhood complete with intelligent conversation, poker games and movie nights. Like a frat. Only without the stupid pranks and rituals and codes of behavior.

Except the Pack did have its own codes of behavior. And its own way of looking at the outside world, which included condescendingly referring to other werewolves as "mutts" and suspecting them all of being too stupid or too weak to avoid the temptation to hunt humans. In that way they were, he suspected, a little too frat-like for him. A little too elitist.

A twig cracked somewhere in the forest. He peered out, but saw only snow and trees.

Oh, sure, Elena, I'll stay out here, alone, after you thought you sensed someone watching us.

Still, if there *was* anyone there, it was probably just the moron who'd slashed their tires. Or a deer. Most likely a deer. In Alaska, he'd noticed that the Pack werewolves could be a little paranoid. Of course, up there, that suspicious nature had saved their lives. Maybe his, too.

He walked around the evergreen, watching, listening and sniffing the air. When a faint scent wafted past, he stiffened. Yep, there was definitely someone out there. It wasn't strong enough for him to tell whether it was the vandal they'd chased, but it was clearly human.

Damn.

Morgan wasn't confrontational by nature. That's how he'd been raised. Avoid contact and avoid trouble. It had served him well in Alaska, where he'd managed to avoid the notice of a group of werewolf-like evolutionary throwbacks called Shifters. More importantly, he'd avoided a group of werewolves who might have claimed to be fully evolved, but it was questionable, given their behavior. They'd been exactly the kind of murdering, raping thugs people expected of werewolves.

He'd known what kind of men they were, and he'd done nothing about it. He felt the guilt—and the shame—of that. Sure, he'd had plenty of excuses. There were half a dozen of them, all career criminals in their prime, never going anywhere alone. If they'd found him, they would have killed him. When Elena and Clay showed up, he'd helped them find and stop them. But he should have done more, done something, done it sooner.

So maybe lying low wasn't always such a good plan. Excellent for self-preservation. Not so good for the conscience.

He squinted into the growing shadows and sniffed again. Yep, there was definitely someone out there. And if he did entertain thoughts of joining the Pack, he couldn't let Clayton Danvers come back and discover that Morgan had hidden and waited for a potential threat to go away. He'd be branded a coward, and if that got out to the werewolf community at large, he might as well high-tail it back to Alaska and hide there.

The scent had vanished, but Morgan knew where it had come from. He headed in that direction, head high, gaze fixed forward, ready to—

Something pressed against the back of his neck. Cold metal. Then he heard the distinct click of a rifle.

Five

So I REPORTED the dead body. I explained that our tires had been slashed and we'd pursued the vandal into the forest. Then I fudged the truth and said we got hit by snow-blindness and ended up farther in than we expected. We were looking for the way out when we thought we spotted someone crouched under an evergreen. We investigated and found a corpse.

Chief Dales rounded up the older officer we'd seen earlier—a guy named Jaggerman—and a younger one named Kent. Then she had to call one of the night shift in to cover the station while we were gone. Apparently, a dead body warranted full departmental support. I'd asked her when was the last time they'd had one—just making conversation on the walk. She hadn't answered. Seemed she meant it when she'd told us to get out of town, and she wasn't too happy that we hadn't listened, even if we had a good excuse.

Contrary to what I'd told her, Clay and I both have a very good sense of direction…aided by a very good sense of smell. So we were able to escort the police right to where we'd left Morgan and the body.

The clearing was empty.

"Morgan?" I called.

Clay shouted louder, voice edged with annoyance. "Morgan!"

No answer. I looked around. I could faintly make out his footsteps, but they'd already filled with falling snow.

Beside me, Clay muttered, "Better not have bolted." He said it too low for the cops to hear. I nodded and motioned for him to subtly start searching. When Morgan had offered to stay behind, I should have considered the possibility he'd decided to bolt. But he'd had a chance to do that while we were all tromping separately through the woods. Maybe being alone just gave him time to think. Or maybe he decided that reporting a dead body was more trouble than he bargained for.

I bent to pull back the branches. "I don't know where he went, but the body is—"

I swore under my breath. The body was gone, too.

"Looks like you've got the wrong spot," Chief Dales said. "Time to tell your friend to invest in a cell phone."

"No, I can definitely smell decomp. This is the place."

"How do you know what decomp smells like?" Jaggerman asked, eyes narrowing.

"We live in the country. There are enough dead things around to recognize the smell."

The officers nodded. That excuse wouldn't fly with someone from the city, but living out here, so close to nature, they knew it was true.

Chief Dales gazed out into the empty forest. "Then I guess we need to go back and organize a search party. For a living guy and a dead one. Though how the hell they went missing together is a mystery I'm not sure I want to solve."

I started to move off, my gaze fixed on Clay, a hundred feet away, waiting for me to come find Morgan. He may have bolted, but he wasn't getting far without a working car. I doubted Westwood even had a cab company.

"We'll look for our friend," I said.

"No, you reported a dead body. You're coming back to the station. You can join the hunt for your friend after you make your statement."

As we walked, we kept our eyes and noses open for any sign of Morgan. I thought I caught a faint whiff of him once, but the scent vanished before I could snag it. I glanced over at Clay. He hadn't detected it—my nose is slightly better. I considered asking if I could handle the statement while Clay went hunting, but Chief Dales didn't exactly seem open to reasonable suggestions. Once again, we made the trek in silence. The younger officer—Kent—tried to start conversation a few times, but glowers from his chief were seconded by Jaggerman's.

Was this just your typically insular village? Either you belong here or they'd rather you kept moving? Not every small community is like that, but I've come across a few, and this region seemed to have more than its share. Clay and I could wear old, casual clothes without a scrap of bling beyond our wedding rings, but there was something about us that screamed "from the city." Maybe it was the luxury SUV we'd rolled into town with. Maybe it was the fact that our clothing didn't bear department store labels. We had money—or, I should say, Jeremy did—and I suppose it shows whether we intend it to or not.

You'd think that wouldn't affect someone like Jessica Dales. She was young, which usually helps alleviate xenophobia. Also, she wasn't local herself, given a casual comment Kent had made. And she didn't quite fit in either, looking more like a TV version of a small town police chief.

Still, she was obviously annoyed that we hadn't followed orders and left town. Maybe it was because we'd gone on to find a dead body, which was missing, totally screwing up her day—and probably her week.

When we walked into the station, I caught a whiff of perspiration strong enough to wipe out everything else. A thirty-something officer behind the desk looked distressed. I presumed the smell came from the guy standing in front of him, a heavy, middle-aged guy in a camouflage jacket, his bald head shining with sweat. A rifle rested across the counter.

"Uh, Chief," the officer said. "Mac here—"

"Got something for you, Jess."

Mac beamed over at Chief Dales, then motioned with a flourish at his trophy. It was Morgan, hands bound behind his back.

"Found this vagrant walking away from a murder scene," Mac said.

Morgan's brows shot up. "Vagrant?"

"Oh, sorry," Mac said sarcastically. "Homeless. Or do we have to say domicile-challenged these days? This ain't Syracuse, boy. You're a vagrant or a drifter. And you should count yourself lucky, because you're about to get three squares a day and a warm cell to sleep in."

As Morgan sputtered, Mac turned back to Chief Dales. "Like I said, found him leaving the scene of a crime. A murder, no less. So I brought him in for you." An almost sheepish look, like a boy presenting a cute girl with a bouquet of wild flowers. "Even brought you the body."

He waved toward an office door to the side. I stepped forward and looked through into what seemed to be the chief's office. There was the decomposing body, in several pieces, atop a garbage bag.

❦

To Chief Dales' credit, she remained calm when she saw a corpse on her desk. Also to her credit, she obviously realized this was a problem—that removing the remains had irrevocably tainted the crime scene. She resisted the urge to explode at Mac, which I'm sure wasn't easy. Instead, she thanked him and nicely explained that, should he find more corpses in the forest, it was really best to just make a note of them for the police. Then she grabbed Kent, with a camera and crime-scene kit, and headed back out, pausing only long enough to make sure Jaggerman knew to call the coroner.

We were forgotten. Which would have been a pleasant surprise, except that we had no place to go. We asked the night duty officer about a garage for our tires, and he said the only mechanic—with the only tow-truck—was currently out on calls. He'd have the guy phone us when he could, but given the weather it would likely be "a while."

"Did I hear you right?" Morgan said as we left. "You *volunteered* to stick around?"

"Doesn't mean *you* need to," Clay said. "Better for us if we don't have to worry about rescuing you a third time."

Morgan's face darkened. Before he could respond, I cut in. "If you'd rather push on, we understand. But I doubt anyone is getting out of town tonight, and we can always use the extra help."

Morgan ignored him. "Help with what? Why are we staying?"

"Because we can't leave and because we have a dead body with chew marks. As long as we're stuck here, we should investigate." I waved at a wall mural of a wolf-man howling at the moon. "Just in case you're not the only werewolf who thought it'd be funny to hang out in Westwood."

Six

PART OF THE Pack's job is to police outside werewolves. You could call it an ethical responsibility to the human world. I do think of it that way. If they don't know what we are, then they can't be prepared to face man-eating mutts. Their law enforcement can't be prepared to find and punish werewolf offenders. Sure, they can treat them as regular murderers, but most man-eaters are at least as savvy as an experienced serial killer. They know where to hunt and how to avoid detection, culling those who won't be missed. Even if they don't, they're leaving partially-eaten bodies, with canine fur and paw-prints. Your typical homicide detective won't look at that and say, "We have a serial killer."

Considering that the favored target of mutts is prostitutes—one of those key "won't be missed" groups—I feel an extra duty to stop man-eaters. Being a woman and a journalist, it's one of my hot-button issues. If the average person vanishes, you get articles and special alerts. If a hooker does, most police departments attribute it to transient living. I know that attitude comes from experience, but it still pisses me off. So if I find an area reporting a lot of missing sex-trade workers, I'll investigate for evidence of a man-eater.

Yet the Pack doesn't hunt man-eaters because it's their civic duty. We do it for the same reason we busted our asses getting to Westwood. Defending the Pack against an exposure threat. I'm constantly scouring the Internet for crimes that could suggest a mutt with a taste for human flesh—or just a taste for killing. I find about a half-dozen possibilities a year. Maybe one will turn up a werewolf culprit. Sometimes none do. There aren't that many of us in North America, so the chance of real trouble is low, but we do check it out.

If I'd found this case on the Internet, would I investigate? Not if it wasn't so close to home. Even then, I wouldn't rush. A corpse with evidence of predation was hardly a sign of werewolves. While we were extra paranoid about potential killings on our own territory, this would have gotten little more than a cursory closer look. But as I'd said to Morgan, we were stuck here anyway. And, admittedly, while I was quite certain a months-old murder had nothing to do with our tires being slashed—or my feelings of being watched—it did bother me enough to decide we shouldn't hurry to leave town.

The first thing I wanted to do was get a really good look at that body. If we were considering a werewolf diner, we needed more than Clay's casual observation. I'd tried to get a better look at the body in the police station, but Chief Dales had closed and locked her office as soon as she realized she had a corpse on display.

Before we'd left, I'd listened in on Officer Jaggerman's phone call to the coroner. He wouldn't be able to get to it right away—he was the town doctor, too, with more appointments before his day ended. He also didn't particularly want a decomposed body in his office, which doubled as his home. They'd decided to temporarily take it to the high school. Whether he planned to work on it there or just keep it there temporarily, I had no idea. Apparently, in Westwood, storing a decomposing body in the school science lab was a perfectly fine solution.

So we needed to pay a visit to the school. Preferably after all the kids were gone. It was nearly five now. I figured we had another hour, to be sure.

We checked in at the local motel. Morgan followed us down the sidewalk. His room was the one past ours, so I thought he would just keep going. He didn't.

When I opened our door and he was still standing there, Clay turned to give him a look.

"You said we were doing this case together," Morgan said.

"Yeah," Clay said. "The case. Not—"

I cut him off. "We're waiting for the school to empty out."

"So we have time to kill."

"Yes," I said, stepping into our room. "Yes, we do."

"You want to grab something at the diner? Food's good."

"Why don't you do that. We're going take a nap."

"He's not five, darling." Clay turned to Morgan. "You need to get lost so we can have sex."

Morgan backed away fast, muttering that he'd return at dusk.

"Subtle," I said to Clay as Morgan hurried off.

"Subtle wasn't working."

He glanced along the row of motel doors, and out at the empty parking lot. Then he hailed Morgan and called, "Looks like we're the only guests checked in. How about you go on over to the diner. Get an early meal."

Morgan seemed ready to protest, caught Clay's look and headed into the parking lot, looking confused.

"See?" Clay said. "Subtle doesn't work."

"He did as you asked."

"Yeah, because he's scared of me. Not because he has the faintest clue why we might not want him in the next room while we're having sex."

"Not because he's slow—because he's young. He's not yet reached that wonderful stage in life where there's no greater gift your roommate can give than offering to take your kids out for an hour."

"I seem to recall we were pretty damned happy when Jeremy left *before* the kids came."

I laughed. "True."

That was the problem with having a permanent housemate. It's not that we'd shock him. Werewolves aren't high on privacy. We run and hunt together whenever we can, and I'd long passed the stage of scrambling for my clothing as soon as I Changed back. And Jeremy has long since stopped opening a closed door—any closed door—without knocking first. The problem is that keeping the door shut doesn't mean he's not going to *hear* what's going on. It's that pesky enhanced hearing. Clay and I aren't particularly loud in bed, but there is… noise. So we need to be careful not to do or say anything that might be a little awkward to recall when sitting across from Jeremy at dinner. Or I'm careful. Clay doesn't care.

But now we had the room—and the motel—to ourselves, with no need to worry how thin the walls were.

As the door closed, Clay tried to grab me around the waist. I danced out of his reach.

"You know what?" I said. "We have an hour, and we're used to making do with a lot less. I should probably do some research first."

I waited for Clay's inevitable growl and pounce.

"You're right." He waved at the bed. "You do that; I'll take a nap."

When I hesitated, he looked over at me.

"What?" he said. "You did want to work, right?"

"Umm..."

"You weren't just saying that to tease me, were you? Expecting me to jump you because I'm a guy, so naturally I want sex a lot more than you do."

Damn.

"Well?" he said. "Do you want to work? Or were you engaging in some highly sexist teasing?"

Damn.

"I...should do some research," I said. "That'd be the responsible, Alpha-elect way to spend a free hour."

"Absolutely."

He strolled to the bed, plunked down and stretched out on his back, eyes closing. "Wake me up if you change your mind."

Damn.

As I started for my laptop, Clay sat up and stripped off his T-shirt.

"Hey," I said.

"What? It's warm in here." He slanted a look my way. "It doesn't bother you, does it?"

I've been seeing him naked for twenty years. Watching him take off his shirt should hardly put my hormones in a tizzy. So I should deny it. Which I would, if I could without so blatantly lying that I feared my nose might grow.

When I didn't answer, Clay chuckled. He undid his belt and slid it out of the loops, then popped the button on his jeans.

"Hey!" I said. "It's not that hot in here."

"Not yet." He glanced over. "Unless you're interested in changing that."

"I'm fine," I growled.

"Well, if that changes at any point, you know where to find me."

He stretched out on the bed again. I admired. I knew I shouldn't, but it was such a nice view, that muscled chest, that faint line of golden hair leading down to—

I turned away. Clay laughed. I continued heading for my laptop. As I walked, I undid my own jeans. I slid them down and kicked them aside. Then I bent down to pick up my laptop, taking my time, giving him a view of his own.

He let out a soft growl. "When did you have time to change into *that*?"

I was wearing my thong. I only own one—bought when I found panty lines showing on a new dress. Of course, I don't wear dresses very often. I didn't wear the thong that often either, despite the fact that I knew Clay liked it. If you've been together long enough you learn that, despite the temptation to wear something your partner likes every day, it'll quickly lose its allure if it becomes everyday wear.

"We were getting low on clean laundry," I said.

"Not that low," he said. "You didn't have time to change before we left, so you must have put it on this morning. What were you planning to do? Strip down tonight and tease me, knowing no way in hell we'd get Jeremy to take the kids out in a snowstorm?"

"No, I thought *we* could go out in a snowstorm."

He rose on his elbows.

"I was planning to ask if you wanted to go for a run after the kids were in bed. Or, if this"—I plucked the thong—"made you decide you weren't so keen on the running part, I'd stashed a sleeping bag and some blankets out there. Cold snow. Warm blankets. Hot sex. I seem to recall you like that."

A growl answered. I turned and bent again. As I did, I unbuttoned my shirt and shrugged it off. Then I picked up the laptop, straightened and turned.

His gaze dropped to my bare breasts. "I see we're *really* low on clean clothes."

"We are."

I could feel him watching as I lay down on the bed and propped myself up on the pillows.

"You go ahead and sleep," I said. "It looks like you could use the rest. In the meantime, since you're obviously not that into it, I'll see if I can find something to amuse me on the Internet. Maybe hot werewolf sex. I hear they have that."

"I've got that right here, too."

I looked over. "Do you?"

"Yep. Just gotta ask." He stretched out, jeans riding down his hips, zipper parting to show what was on offer. "Or take."

Damn.

I glanced at the clock. I could hold out, but time was ticking. One thing you learn in marriage is the art of give and take.

This time, I took.

Seven

THE STORM WAS blasting for real now, wind and snow whipping around us, the sky dark. We stood outside the high school, hidden behind a massive sign that read. "Football Semi-Finals Saturday! Go Werewolves!" It looked like a typical country school—a one-floor cinderblock, with no redeeming architectural features. The simple layout would make infiltration easy. So would the parking lot with only two cars, both almost buried under snow, making me wonder if the owners had just left them there.

I glanced at Morgan. "I'm going to have you stand guard. Come closer to the side door with us, then watch the lot and whistle if you see anything. Don't engage; just whistle."

We walked around the side of the school. Morgan followed. When we reached the doors, they were flush with the building, leaving him no recess to hide in. So he just stood there, at the corner.

"Better take cover," I whispered.

"Yeah," Clay said. "We don't want to spring you from the cop shop again."

Morgan scowled and stalked off to hide behind a cluster of evergreens. When he was gone, Clay examined the door, then looked around.

"Too exposed," he said.

I nodded and waved to the back. We found a better door around there. Not only was it recessed, but it backed onto the football field, which was surrounded by forest.

As Clay checked the lock, I said, "You could go a little easier on him. The Pack needs wolves, and he seems like a good kid."

"Yeah, but if he can't take direction and criticism? Pack's the wrong place for him."

"He's taking direction just fine. It's the criticism that's causing problems."

Clay heaved on the door until the lock snapped. Then he opened it an inch, inhaling and listening. He seemed to be ignoring me, but I knew he was processing. Struggling to reconcile instinct and logic.

He was capable of being nicer. Hell, our kids have never heard a critical word from him. Disapproving, yes. But a gentle growl and nudge in the right direction, rather than a snarl and snap. He'd do the same with any Pack child, I'm sure. That's the wolf in him.

But a grown wolf like Morgan required a sterner hand. He'd get the snarl and snap, reminding him of his place and booting him into it. Once Clay was sure Morgan understood that, he'd get the growls and nudges, like Noah and Reese did, more gently shaping their behavior as he taught them everything they needed to know to survive and flourish as a werewolf.

"He's more than ten years older than Noah," I said. "At least five years older than Reese. He isn't a kid, and he doesn't appreciate being treated like one."

Clay closed the door and looked over. "You want him in the Pack?"

"I want to have the chance to evaluate that."

Clay's chin dipped. "Fair enough. I'll take it down a notch."

"Thank you."

"But if he screws up—"

I lifted a hand. That's all I needed to do. We'd already taken a chance, coming here to help Morgan. If he messed up another time, he'd be escorted to the state border and told—in detail—what would happen to him if he ever trespassed on Pack territory again.

We entered the school. It was, as I'd noted from peering in, a very simple layout. Two corridors ran lengthwise and a short one connected those two to the front and back doors. The first hallway was empty.

Clay headed along the short connecting corridor. I followed. When we reached the corner, I peered down the long front hall to see a woman in a nurse's uniform. She sat at a table doing a crossword. Standing guard over the body? Looked like it. Smelled like it, too, from the faint scent of decomp wafting past on the furnace heat.

I backed us up to the rear corridor, the empty one. We went down it and found the third door led into a classroom decorated with fading DNA and cell posters. A door at the back was conveniently labeled "lab." It was locked, but Clay's sharp twist on the handle fixed that.

Clay checked through the door. I glimpsed a sliver of the lab. When I stepped to the side, I could see the main door to the hall. It was half open, showing the corner of the nurse's table.

Clay opened the door a little more. He peeked in, then withdrew and shut it.

"Body's right there," he whispered. "If she gets up and looks in, she'll see us."

I took a deep breath. "Can you manage a quick examination?"

He nodded. Clay's a cultural anthropologist, not a forensic one, but he's done a fair bit of cross-reading and studying. He's not an expert, but he's a damned sight closer to it than I am.

Clay went in. He crept soundlessly to the left, where I could see the edge of the examining table. Then he bent over the body, pencil in hand, to poke and prod at the corpse.

I listened for any noise from the nurse's post. She didn't move. Then Clay stopped, head tilting. I caught the sound a split-second after he did. Morgan's whistle.

Clay hurried back into the classroom with me. A moment later, we heard the faint whoosh of the front doors opening. Then the louder sound of footsteps. Boots. Heavy. A grown man, I was guessing. Alone. His footsteps approached the nurse's station.

"Hey, Miz Morrison. Doc got you standing guard?"

The voice sounded vaguely familiar. I motioned for Clay to crack the door open. He did and we caught the scent of Officer Kent.

"He does," the nurse replied. "At least until he figures out how to do the autopsy here. Or bring that thing back to the office without making every patient sick from the smell."

"Well, you can take a break from the smell yourself. Why don't you head over to the corner store and grab a coffee? I'll be here awhile. Chief wants pictures."

"Didn't she get enough earlier?"

"Apparently not. You know how she is."

"Thorough," the nurse said. "Which is more than anyone could say for Chief Lyons."

Kent murmured something under his breath that could be taken as agreement, but I got the feeling he'd rather his boss was a little less dedicated to her job. I wondered how long she'd been chief. Probably not very, which might explain her attitude. The new girl on the block, working to prove she deserved her post.

There was scuffling as the nurse gathered her things, clearly eager to be gone. As Kent walked her to the door, he asked if the janitor was around.

"Snowed in, last I heard," the nurse said. "I'm hoping he'll show up soon. Doc said I can leave if he does. Otherwise, I'm stuck here until he's done his evening appointments."

As they talked, Clay leaned over and whispered, "I got enough."

I looked back at the classroom door. "I think we'd make more noise leaving than staying. We'll go as soon as Kent settles in."

Clay nodded. Footsteps sounded in the hall again. I watched through the crack as Kent entered the science lab, big camera in hand. He walked to the table. Then he stopped and seemed to be listening, as if waiting to see if the nurse would come back. After a moment, he laid the big camera on the edge of the table. Then he started taking photos…with his cell phone.

Clay grunted. I nodded. For at least ten minutes, Kent took shots, from every possible angle. Then he grabbed the big camera and snapped a few pictures, with nowhere near as much care as he'd taken in getting the ones for his private collection.

When he finished, he stood over the body, staring at it. Then he reached out and—

The front doors creaked open. Kent shoved his cell phone into his pocket, picked up the camera and strode from the lab.

"That was fast," he called.

"Polly closed shop early," the nurse answered. "Too much snow and not enough business, I guess, but…"

We slipped away as they talked.

WE WERE WAITING for Officer Kent when he exited the school. He'd arrived in what must have been his personal vehicle—a pickup. Not surprising, given that I was pretty sure he was here on his own time, pursuing his own interests. What interests could involve taking photographs of a decaying corpse? Several. None that he'd add to an online dating profile.

He could plan to sell them online. Yes, there are people who'll buy that sort of thing. Using his position to sell macabre photographs of crime scene evidence violated his professional obligations—and made him a bottom-feeding creep—but it wasn't as bad as the possibility he wanted them to satisfy his own perverse interest in dead bodies. But the most heinous explanation was the one I liked best, because it would mean our killer definitely wasn't a werewolf—he was a small-town police officer who couldn't resist more photographic trophies of his handiwork.

We waited behind the sign as Kent crossed the parking lot. While he was distracted clearing snow from his vehicle, I motioned for Morgan to loop around behind him. Clay and I set out. Kent didn't notice us until I called, "Officer?"

He jumped and swung the brush up like a weapon. Then, as snow crunched behind him, he turned to see Morgan approaching from the other direction.

I smiled. "Seems like a never-ending task today, doesn't it?"

"Wh-what?"

I motioned at the snow brush.

"Oh, right."

I stopped in front of him. Clay halted behind me.

"I heard the body was here." I waved at the school, then at the camera around his neck. "Taking pictures for Chief Dales?"

"Uh, yes."

"Hope they help."

I started heading past him, Clay beside me.

"I'll let her know you're hard at work," I called back.

"What?" He scrambled over to us so fast he slid in the snow.

"We're just heading to the station to see how things are going."

"No, umm..." He looked from me to Clay, then cleared his throat. "I wouldn't waste your time. Chief Dales isn't at the station. She's off trying to ID the victim."

"Oh? They haven't made an ID yet? Well, it shouldn't take long. You can't have many missing people in this town."

He hesitated. He knew he shouldn't tell me anything, but he didn't want me going to the station either.

He moved closer, lowering his voice conspiratorially. "Between you and me? I don't think she's going to make an ID. Guy's obviously a drifter. We get them through here all the time. He wouldn't be the first to disappear."

"No?"

He shrugged. "It happens everywhere."

Actually, no, it doesn't. Not in a place the size of Westwood.

Eight

WAS KENT SERIOUS about drifters going missing in Westwood? Or was he just saying that so we'd back off? There was an easy way to find out. Research.

First, we needed to notify Jeremy. I'd called him earlier, after the local mechanic finally phoned to say he was stuck handling a pile-up on the highway and wouldn't be back to town tonight—he lived ten miles away. I'd told Jeremy we wouldn't be home and asked him to break it to the kids. Now I was phoning to update him and say goodnight to them.

We usually Skype with the kids. Ever since they discovered they could see us, too, they weren't going back to regular calls. But the Internet here was slow, meaning it would be an exercise in frustration. So Clay used my cell phone to talk to them while I started my research. Morgan was at the diner grabbing take-out for all of us.

Clay was still on the phone when I saw Morgan pass the window. Then a rap sounded at our door.

"Come in!" I called.

"Yep, that's Mommy," Clay said. "She's…doing some work while we're stuck here. I'm going to pass over the phone to her. Dinner's arrived, so I want you to keep her busy until I finish it all, okay?"

I heard Kate giggling as he handed me the phone.

"Hey, guys," I said. "What's up?"

They were on the speaker-phone at Stonehaven. That's something we learned from Skype—calls home work a lot better when the kids aren't battling for the receiver. They both chattered away, telling me about the Clue tournament they'd played with Jeremy and the phone call from Uncle Nick, who'd promised to bring Reese and Noah up for a weekend of snowshoeing and cross-country skiing.

They didn't complain once. Didn't whine once. Didn't argue once. I should have been happy about that. But there was this little part of me that worried they were being on their best behavior because they suspected we'd fled to escape them. I was probably overreacting. They'd just worked through their cabin fever and slid back into being their usual happy selves. But it didn't keep me from feeling guilty. I'm really good at that.

I promised we'd be home tomorrow. Even if we still had work to do, Westwood was close enough to home for us to make the drive and spend the night at Stonehaven. We just needed to get the damned vehicle fixed. Jeremy said that if it looked as if that wouldn't happen tomorrow, he'd rent another SUV in Syracuse and pick us up. Everyone seemed happy with that solution.

I was wrapping up when Morgan asked Clay if I'd found any more possible murder victims. Clay motioned him to silence and jabbed a finger at the phone. To his credit, he didn't back that up with a scowl. Just a stern look. Which was as close to "being nice" as I could hope for.

"Sorry," Morgan murmured. "Kids with super-hearing. That must be fun. So, did she find what she was, uh, looking for?"

I signed off and started fixing a plate from the food containers covering the bed.

"Kent was right," I said. "This place is a regular Bermuda Triangle for drifters. In the last five years, three have been reported missing in the region. I can imagine how many more *weren't* reported."

"Preying on those who won't be noticed or missed. That's a serial killer m.o., isn't it?"

"Man-eaters, too."

Morgan shrugged. "Same thing."

I shook my head as I swallowed a bite of chicken. "Obviously a repeat man-eater is a serial killer, using the strictest definition of the term. And certainly some are classic serial killers. They kill because they enjoy it. But some just screw up."

"Repeatedly," Clay muttered.

I nodded. "Because they don't have a family or a Pack or anyone to teach them not to Change around humans until they can control the urge to see them as prey."

"But it *could* be a human serial killer," Morgan said.

"Yes," I said. "If so, it's an unusual one. All three missing persons are young men—late teens into twenties. Young guys on the road, looking for work, and a place to call home. Not your usual serial killer prey, but not unheard of."

"So you think this is the work of a man-eater? What'd you learn from the body?"

"He matches the pattern of the missing drifters," Clay said. "Male. Young, but past adulthood. Definite predation. *Major* predation—not something taking a nibble. But a large predator would usually scatter body parts, taking pieces home for later. Everything seemed intact except for that missing hand."

"Then it could be a werewolf."

"Living this close to us? For years? Possible, I guess. But I doubt it."

"Which won't stop us from investigating," I said. "Man-eater or not, we've got people disappearing a little too close to home. Especially if we have partly-eaten bodies." I glanced out the window at the darkness. "Time to see if we can sniff out any more corpses."

THE SNOW HAD stopped falling a while before we headed out, leaving desolate streets without so much as a set of tire imprints, as if everyone had retreated home after dinner and stayed there. Forest bordered the whole north edge of town, so we didn't need to walk far to reach it.

Even with nightfall, it was easier to see than it had been this afternoon. The quarter moon shone from a nearly cloudless sky. With enhanced night vision, that lit things to near-daylight, even inside the tree line.

The forest was silent and still. No sign of footprints or snowmobile tracks. No scent of people or gasoline fumes.

"Is it hunting season?" Morgan asked as we trekked into the forest.

"Deer," Clay said. "Maybe turkey. Can't remember exactly when that ends. Depends on the location."

"Do they hunt either at night?"

"Sunrise to sunset legally," I said. "It's iffy at dusk, but we're usually safe running."

"I'm actually asking because of those guys I heard in the forest last night. It was too late for hunters and I didn't smell snowmobiles. I was wondering what they were doing out there."

"Lots of reasons people go into the woods at night," Clay said. He paused, softening his snap by adding, "But if you hear the voices again in town, let us know. Might be worth figuring out what they were up to."

"Looks like a clearing over there," I said, waving. "Good place to Change."

"I'll stand guard. Morgan—"

"Find my own spot. Got it." He stepped into the clearing ahead of me. "How about just over there—"

He stopped. I followed his finger to see a small animal pelt hanging from a tree. I took another step into the clearing and looked around to see more tiny pelts hanging from trees marked with a familiar symbol.

"We saw these earlier," I said to Clay. "The symbol, not the skins. They were on trees in another clearing, back near where I found the body. I was going to show you photos, just out of curiosity. But apparently it's more than a one-off. It could have something to do with the men Morgan heard in the forest."

"Maybe. The pelts are moles, voles, mice…No ritual significance I can think of there."

He flipped over a pelt and shone a penlight on it. On the back, someone had burned a crook and flail into the skin.

Nine

I WENT FIRST. CLAY had started preferring that. It was part of the transition to our new positions. When I became Alpha, he would be my bodyguard. It wasn't the most comfortable shift, for either of us. We'd always been partners, and I'd taken pride in that—my mate was the most powerful werewolf in the country, yet he didn't feel the need to shove me behind him, where it was safe. He knew that I was safe at his side, able to protect myself—and him, if necessary. But that didn't work for the Alpha and her beta. When it came to plotting and planning, I had to step forward and he had to step back. When it came to matters of safety, the situation reversed. So when we Changed these days, he'd often "suggest" that I go first. That way, if danger struck while he was mid-Change, I'd be in wolf form, better able to protect myself.

I entered the thicket and Changed. It hurt like hell. That part is always the same. Always will be, sadly.

When I finished, I took a moment to ground myself and rest. Most werewolves do. We have to—the shift to another reality is always jarring. Clay is, of course, the exception. There seems to be no discordance for him. He does need to rest, but he rarely bothers, too eager to get out and run.

That meant that it wouldn't be long before he was finished, so I had to prepare. While he began his Change, I examined the playing field. Then I made my move. I ran about a dozen strides away, flying through the snow, feeling the exhilarating cold of it chase away the last aches of the Change. Then I stopped short. I tore around in circles, ripping up the snow, rolling in it. Making a mess, basically. Then I hunkered down, muzzle aimed at the tree line just beyond the clearing, where we'd trampled the snow coming in. I checked my trajectory, crouched and sprang, flying clear over the unbroken snow and past the tree line.

I looked back at my handiwork. A straight running path from the thicket where we Changed ending in that ripped-up patch. It could look like a fight, but there were no other scents. I wouldn't worry him like that. He'd see it and sniff it and think I'd just been goofing around. And then? Well, then I vanished. Just vanished. No sign of where I'd gone. A straight trail to an empty trodden patch, surrounded by unbroken snow.

I chuffed, pleased with myself. Then I crept to the other side of the thicket. As planned, I was downwind of him, where he couldn't smell me. I settled in to wait, head on my paws, tail curled around me. Inside the thicket, I could hear Clay finishing up. I could see him, too, yellow fur bright through the brush.

He got to his feet and started out the way he'd come in. Then he stopped. I could imagine him there, looking at the track-story I'd left, puzzling it out. I wriggled lower. With my pale fur, I'd blend with the snow. If he couldn't see me or smell me or hear me…I resisted the urge to give a chuckling growl.

Clay stepped from the thicket, vanishing from view. I waited. His steps were silent in the soft snow and as much as I strained, I couldn't hear him. Was he just standing there, puzzling? Had I given him enough time to recover from the Change? Was he fair game yet? I lifted my hindquarters, preparing to race up behind him and pounce.

I was just about to launch when a yellow blur tore around the thicket. Coming straight at me. No, that wasn't—He couldn't possibly—

I tried to leap out of the way, but it was too late, and he barreled into me, sending me flying. Then, before I could scramble up, he was the one pouncing. He pinned me, teeth gripping the loose ruff around my neck as he held me down, growling and shaking me.

I sighed and let my paws slide out from under me, admitting defeat. He released me and started backing off. I played submissive—head down, ears flat, tail lowered—while I bunched my legs, ready to—

He pounced again, knocking me on my side this time. I was the one getting hold of his ruff, though, grabbing and growling as we tumbled through the woods, mowing down innocent saplings.

I finally escaped, sprang up and started to run. Just then, Morgan stepped out from his Changing place across the clearing. I made the mistake of pausing to glance over and got plowed down by Clay. He hit me in the side and knocked me flying into the snow. Then he turned to Morgan.

Clay lowered his head. Classic stand-off stance, but he wasn't growling and his ears weren't back, meaning he was just goofing around. Given Morgan's experience with real wolves, he should recognize that, but his expression said he wasn't so sure...and really didn't think he should take a chance.

Finally, Morgan's nerve broke and he took a slow step back. Clay charged. He hit him square in the chest, nearly flipping him backward. Morgan went down. Clay zoomed back to me, paws spinning, spitting up snow in his wake. I chuffed and shook my head.

I glanced over at Morgan. He was on his feet, shaking off snow. His gaze was fixed on Clay. Still evaluating his intent. I resisted the urge to intercede. It's damned near impossible to communicate "he's kidding" in wolf form. Morgan would figure it out eventually, and he seemed to do just that when Clay let him approach without knocking him flying again.

Clay nudged my flank.

I gave him a look to say, "If I stand, are you going to let me *stay* standing?"

He exhaled, breath streaming, and backed up. I slowly rose, flicking my tail and my ears. Then I charged. He feinted out of the way. I nearly plowed into a tree. When I turned around, I swore he was laughing. Morgan, too.

I swished my tail and snorted, then pulled myself up and growled to say playtime was over. Clay rolled his eyes to say I was only ending it because I was losing. Then he set out, racing through the snow. I loped up beside him, Morgan falling in behind.

We only ran long enough to take off the edge that play-fighting hadn't dulled. Then we slowed, fanning out, sniffing the air and pausing for a closer sniff at large evergreens. We'd been out there for maybe an hour when I caught a scent. I motioned to Clay and he lifted his muzzle, then shook his head. The scent was too faint for him.

I followed the smell to a spruce. Branches fanned the ground. Carefully, I pawed one aside. The smell stayed faint, almost hidden by the astringent odor of the needles. I pushed my head into the dark cavity under the branches. It took a moment for my eyes to adjust. When they did, I saw white bone. A skeletal arm encased in a ragged sleeve.

The skeleton's hand was missing. As I pushed farther under the tree, I could see other parts were missing too, including the skull. Did scavengers often make off with skulls? I couldn't recall encountering that—like the hands, there wasn't much "meat" there.

I eased back for a more critical look at the body. It'd been reduced to clothing-covered bones. The clothes were ripped—too badly for a struggle, suggesting predation. It looked like male clothing. The body seemed small, too. Not child-small, but not adult-sized either. On both counts, though, I was just guessing. So I backed up and let Clay in for a look.

He spent a few minutes examining the remains. Then he came out. In wolf-form, he couldn't tell me what he thought, obviously, just gestured that he was done and we could move on.

We did that, making a mental note of our surroundings, then heading out in search of other bodies. Yet if there were more, it quickly became apparent that they were either a lot further in or too old for me to smell.

I stopped to tell the guys we should head back. When I looked around, though, I only saw Clay's golden fur. I threw back my head and howled. After a moment, a distant yip from Morgan replied.

Clay chuffed and shook his head. I howled again. Morgan yipped back. Damn it, when I called, he was supposed to come. Having to go after him was really not going to impress Clay.

I didn't glance over to see Clay's expression. I didn't dare. Just gave one last howl, edged with anger, then set off after Morgan.

Ten

We found Morgan at the foot of a steep hillside. He was standing by a clump of bushes, staring up at a pie pan hanging from a branch. The pan twisted in the breeze, glinting in the moonlight. Great. How the hell was I supposed to convince Clay that Morgan could be Pack material if he was distracted by every shiny object he saw?

He didn't even seem to notice us until I let out a chuff, and he glanced over, casually, as if he'd heard us all along, but had really been more interested in the pie plate. I sighed.

He nosed around the bushes for a moment, then looked over, head tilted as if to say, "Well, are you coming?"

To do what? Join his rapt contemplation of baking tins? I grunted. He yipped, then dove through the bushes…and disappeared into the hillside.

Oh.

Clay bounded over, stuck his head through the bushes, then pushed in until the tip of his tail vanished. I followed.

It seemed that the bushes blocked the entrance to a cave. The pie plate must have been someone's way of marking it. When I got inside, I smacked muzzle-first into Clay's rear end. He chuffed an apology, nails clicking on stone as he stepped further into the inky blackness.

It was nearly complete darkness, only slivers of moonlight managing to get past the entrance. I backed out and held down one of the biggest bushes under my paw. When I did, moonlight flooded into the cave. Inside, Morgan dipped his muzzle as if in thanks. When he started nosing the floor, exploring, Clay let out a low growl.

Morgan looked up, confused. Clay head-butted him toward me. More confusion. I released the bushes a little, then stepped on them again and jerked my head toward him. It took a moment, but he figured out what I meant. He sighed, came to the mouth and took over the job of holding down the branches while I went into the cave for a look.

I suppose I should feel bad about that. After all, he *did* discover it. And I suppose it's a testament to how long I've been a werewolf that I didn't feel very guilty at all. It was simple hierarchy. He'd get his look around…after we got ours.

We'd been standing in the mouth of the cave. It was narrow, which is why we'd smacked into each other. Now Clay squeezed to the side to let me through first. Again, hierarchy, not chivalry. That feels a little strange sometimes—taking precedence over my mate, my partner—but it's starting to feel less weird as I manage to disentangle the Alpha-elect part of my life from the rest. We're fine as long as the unbalance in power doesn't extend beyond this, and I can be damned sure Clay's never going to allow that.

I walked into a second, bigger chamber. It stank of wood smoke, as if someone had used it for a bonfire. Everything was dark for a moment, as Clay came through the mouth and blocked the moonlight. Then he stepped aside and I looked around.

There was a moment where I thought I'd found some ancient cave painted by Neolithic man. In my defense, it was only a brief moment. I may not have Clay's background, but I know we're a long way from anyplace with Neolithic cave paintings. When my eyes adjusted, I could see these weren't even mock paintings. They were symbols, sketched with what looked like chalk and soot.

They weren't the same symbols I'd seen on the trees, but some looked similar. As I stepped forward for a better look, Clay nudged my flank and whined. Telling me to stop. I looked over at him. He bent his muzzle to the cave floor and nosed what looked like a white, tubular rock. Then he jerked his head toward the rest of the floor.

We were on the edge of a ritual circle, adorned with more symbols. In the center, ashes and burned wood explained the smell. There were dark splotches just to my left. I carefully picked my way over to them. Dark red. I lowered my nose and inhaled. It was hard to get past the smell of smoke that permeated the cave, but eventually I detected blood. Animal or human, I couldn't tell—they were too old—but it was definitely blood.

Clay nosed the white rock again, then gestured to a pile of them in the middle of the circle. I walked in, being careful not to step on the markings or the dried blood. When I reached the pile, I could see they weren't stones at all. They were finger bones.

Was this where those missing hands ended up? If so, they hadn't been scavenged. These bones were bright white and smelled faintly of sodium hypochlorite. Boiled clean and bleached.

I needed a better look at this. Which required fingers, a camera and a penlight. Time to Change back. I communicated that to Clay, then had him hold down the bushes while I let Morgan take a look around before we started the long run back to our clothing.

I TOOK PICTURES while Clay examined the symbols. Morgan hung back and watched.

"I'm not recognizing anything," Clay said. "The symbols look like a mix of a few things. That could suggest a supernatural ritual, not a human one."

I nodded. "The bones and blood point to necromancy. The symbols look more witch or sorcerer. I'll send the photos to Jaime and Paige."

I was snapping a picture when my cell phone beeped, telling me I had a message. It was a text from Chief Dales asking us to stop by the station. She'd sent it at nine. I checked my watch. It was just past ten.

I told Clay and Morgan, then said, "We'll swing out that way and pop in, but I'm guessing she'll be gone for the night."

"Are we reporting this?" Morgan waved at the cave.

I shook my head. "Not this and not the other body. I'd like to report the body, at least, but finding two in one day is a little much. We'll have to hope they conduct a thorough search of their own and find it." I looked at the cave. "And hope they don't find *this* until we figure out what the hell it means."

So what *did* that cave mean? I could be optimistic and say it had nothing to do with the dead bodies. Sure, it was a little coincidental finding corpses missing hands, then hands missing a corpse. Maybe someone had found hands carried off by animals and decided to boil them for ritualistic parts rather than turn them over to the police. You know, you're out, walking your dog through the woods, he brings back human hands and you think, "Huh, I could use those." Perfectly plausible.

Actually, if the dog-walker was a necromancer, it *was* possible. They needed human remains for rituals, and they didn't require fresh ones, so they got creative. Jeremy's longtime girlfriend, Jaime Vegas, was a necromancer, so I knew a little more about it than I did other supernatural types. She did use "bits-and-bobs" from dead bodies, most of them ancient, but she'd never just claim random body parts found lying about. And she didn't use blood. Dried flesh and old bones signified death, which was the domain of the necromancer. Blood signifies life.

It seemed more likely to be spell-casters. Witch, sorcerer or maybe one of the rarer and weaker magical races. Ninety-nine percent of magic has nothing to do with ritual sacrifice. But there is that one percent. The darkest spells, shunned by most practitioners. The highest level of magic, requiring the highest level of sacrifice—a human life. But I wasn't sure the blood was human. It could be animal sacrifice...paired with human remains from someone conveniently killed under completely separate circumstances.

Yes, any explanation other than a ritual murder was a stretch. A big one. No matter how rare it was in the supernatural world, I had to entertain the very strong possibility that's exactly what this was.

I expected to arrive at the police station and find it shuttered. Or, at the very least, nearly dark, with only the night officer on duty. Instead, all the windows were ablaze and I could hear voices from a hundred feet away. It seemed every set of footprints on the street led straight to the station doors. The only cars in sight—three of them—were parked out front.

"Party at the cop shop?" Morgan said.

"Something's going on. I just hope Chief Dales' message didn't mean 'get your asses over here fast because we have a situation.'"

"No reason it would involve us," Clay said.

"I hope not."

I decided to send Morgan back to the motel. I wasn't sure how far news of his escapade had traveled, but given my experience with small towns, the answer was "far." Best to leave him out of this.

Clay and I stepped inside to find three people hanging out in the small foyer. Just standing there. They moved aside for us, but didn't say a word. I kicked the snow off my boots and opened the interior door.

Officer Jaggerman was manning the front desk. Three more people stood in front of it, all leaning in, holding Jaggerman's attention. A couple in their late thirties hung back, casting anxious glances at us. Another in their forties sat to the side. I could hear Chief Dales' voice coming through her closed office door. Talking to Kent, it sounded like. Or hiding in there with him. I wasn't sure I blamed her.

Two of the people in front of Jaggerman seemed to be a couple. Maybe my age. Latino, like the younger couple to the side. With them was a man of about thirty-five, balding and beefy, a worn Westwood Werewolves team jacket straining over his broad chest.

"I demand to see that body," the woman was saying, loud enough to make my ears ring.

"It won't help, Mrs. Rivera," Jaggerman said. "You won't be able to tell if it's—"

"Are you telling me I won't recognize my own son?"

"The body is in…" Jaggerman swallowed, "poor condition."

The guy in the football jacket laid his hand on Mrs. Rivera's arm. "If it is Ricky, you'll know as soon as they do, Maria. Some of the other team parents"—he gestured at the sitting couple—"have volunteered to take turns staying here all night until Jess has an answer."

As if on cue, Chief Dales' door opened. She walked out, papers in hand.

"No one needs to stay," she said. "I just got Doc's preliminary report. As we thought, the body is that of a man in his early twenties, too old to be Ricky. Even more conclusively, there were several tattoos. That means it definitely isn't your son."

Chief Dales walked over and offered a few quieter words of sympathy. I could tell she was struggling. I recognized that look—I can feel deeply for people, but I have trouble expressing it, especially to those I don't know well. Dales' sentiment did seem genuine, though.

Mrs. Rivera didn't appreciate the effort. She muttered something under her breath, then stalked out, leaving her husband and the guy in the team jacket hurrying after her. None of them paid any attention to us. Nor did Chief Dales as she walked to the front desk, pages in hand.

"Doc confirmed it looks like homicide," she said to Jaggerman. "I've compiled a list of persons of interest. All our local recluses."

"You want me to take a run at them tonight?"

"Your shift ended two hours ago, Phil. I told you to go home then, and after that visit, I bet you're wishing you listened."

He chuckled. "No kidding." He glanced at us. He'd looked over earlier, but been caught up with the Riveras. "Uh, Jess, we have—"

"I'll leave these addresses here," she said. "Take Wes in the morning and see who you can round up for questioning."

I approached the desk as she set the pages on it. "You texted me?"

She glanced over sharply, as if startled. A little *too* startled. As if she'd only been pretending she hadn't noticed us.

"Oh," she said. "You didn't need to stop in."

"The message said—"

"I just wanted to know if you're spending the night in Westwood."

"We are. No luck getting our tires fixed with all the storm calls. The mechanic is coming by in the morning."

"Good. You're staying at the Red Cedar, I'm guessing?" She struggled for a tired smile. "Only place in town."

"It is."

She nodded. "I may have more questions in the morning. If I don't stop by before you leave, give me a ring."

"All right."

I started to turn away.

"Grab yourselves a coffee before you head out," she called. "It's a cold night." Then, to Jaggerman, "Phil? Got a few things for you to sign."

They disappeared into her office as I was pouring a coffee. She shut the door behind them. I sidled back to the front desk and glanced down at the pages she'd left out. Clay came up beside me.

"A list of the local loners?" I said. "Otherwise known as a list of potential mutts or supernaturals involved in nefarious business."

"Handy."

"No kidding."

I took out my phone. He stood guard as I snapped photos of the pages.

Eleven

I GOT OUTSIDE THE police station before I took a sip of the coffee. It tasted like roasted tree bark. I prepared to dump it into the snow.

"Uh-uh," Clay said. "We've got a long night. You're going to need that."

He was right. The best time to investigate this list was while it was dark enough to skulk around. And before the local cops tackled the list themselves. While I was reasonably sure we didn't have a man-eating werewolf here, it was a possibility.

Even if it was another supernatural, I couldn't just walk away. I was the werewolf delegate to the interracial council, and one of our duties is to guard against exposure threats of any kind. I don't do a lot of that—handling werewolves is quite enough, and the others are happy to leave me to that. But if this turned out to be a witch or a sorcerer conducting human sacrifice, I needed to find the culprit before the police did.

So I choked down half the coffee as fast as I could manage. We were heading toward the motel when a woman's voice called, "You there!"

We turned to see Mrs. Rivera bearing down on us while her husband scrambled from their parked car.

"Maria!" he called.

We waited until she planted herself in front of us. "I saw you at the police station. Then I remembered someone said it was a couple of strangers who found the body. A young couple."

We weren't that young. In fact, we were probably older than she was. True, with a werewolf's slow aging, we looked in our thirties, but I wouldn't call that "young." I wasn't arguing, though.

"Yes, it was us," I said. "We were hiking—"

"Maria." It was the other man from the station, the one in the football jacket. He came up beside her and lowered his voice. "They just found the body. They didn't have anything to do with it."

"Of course they didn't," she snapped. "They only arrived today. I'm not a fool. I just wanted to ask if it could be him."

She held out a photo of a teenage boy. He was heavy-set and soft, and probably looked younger than he was. I would have guessed thirteen, but he wore a football uniform, so he had to be in high school.

I stared at the photo. He was grinning at the camera. He looked so happy. So proud of that uniform. So young. So damned young. When had he disappeared? *How* had he disappeared?

"You recognize him," she whispered.

I shook my head. "I'm sorry. It's just..." I looked up at her. "He looks very happy. I'm so sorry."

The man took the photo. "And I'm sorry," he said to me. "We're all very upset, as you can imagine. This...discovery has only brought it all back." He held out his free hand, first to Clay, who had to be nudged to shake it, then to me. "Tom Hanlon. I'm a teacher up at the high school. I coach the football team."

I introduced us.

"We'll let you get on with your night," he said, putting an arm around Mrs. Rivera's shoulders as he handed back the photo.

"No!" She knocked his arm away and turned to us. "Are you sure it couldn't have been—?"

"Jess said the body has tattoos," Coach Hanlon said. "Ricky didn't have tattoos."

"I don't care what she said. I don't know *how* she got that job. Or who she slept with."

"Maria!" The coach's eyes widened. "Jessica Dales is the chief of police because she was better qualified—"

"This is my boy, Ricky," she said, shoving the photo at me again. "He went missing just after last Thanksgiving."

I shook my head. "The man we found was older and died much more recently. It wasn't your son. I'm sorry."

It took a few minutes—and her husband's help—to get Mrs. Rivera back to the car. I didn't try to escape until she was gone. Clay didn't either. We just stood there, waiting. Even then, we walked slowly as the car drove away, not wanting to seem like we had better things to do. The woman had lost her child. I couldn't imagine what that was like—didn't dare try.

"The guy we found this afternoon definitely wasn't him," Clay murmured as the rear lights of their car faded in the distance. "But the second body? The smaller one? Hard to judge exactly, but I'd say it's been there about a year."

"I know."

A couple of hours later we were hiding in the forest watching an old woman with a rifle stalk around her dilapidated cabin, gaze on the ground as she searched for footprints. She didn't find any—I'd been careful to approach only as close as I could get without leaving the forest. She stomped back to her porch and stood there, faded nightgown whipping around her spindly legs.

"You better run!" she shouted. "This is private property, you hear? Don't want no damn hunters. Or kids. Or sledders. Or..."

The list went on, covering every possible type of person who might break the sacred seal of privacy she'd created out here.

"Aliens?" Morgan said.

"Bet she's been beamed up a time or two," Clay muttered.

"It's like something out of an old hillbilly cartoon," I said, marveling as I watched. "I thought the last cabin was bad."

"They're all bad," Clay said. "The only difference is whether they're half-crazy or all the way there."

He was right. We'd checked out four cabins so far. With two, I'd barely gotten close enough for a good sniff before someone came thundering out, as if they could sense trespassers. The other two had been sleeping—passed out drunk, it looked like.

"Is every paranoid survivalist in America living in these woods?" I said.

"Only half," Morgan said. "The rest are in Alaska. I think I bumped into most of them."

"Maybe I'll let you take the next one, then."

We waited until the old woman went inside, then we set out again. Finding the people on Chief Dales' list was getting tougher with every name we crossed off. The first three had been locals in town. That was easy enough. But these past four were forest cabins and only the first was even on a road. To find the rest, Dales had listed coordinates. We'd taken the portable GPS unit from Jeremy's SUV. It still wasn't easy.

We continued walking for about ten minutes before I could make out a distant, unlit cabin. We veered to the side, approaching from the forest.

"Do you want to handle this one?" I asked Morgan.

He didn't answer. Just spun and wrenched Clay's arm, yanking him hard. Clay caught Morgan's wrist and threw him down on his back, then loomed over him.

"Don't ever—"

Morgan cut him off by pointing to the side. We both looked to see metal almost buried in the snow. Watching Clay, Morgan rose, then reached for a nearby stick, waved us back and poked at the metal. A bear trap sprang, jaws snapping the stick in two.

"That's another thing I saw a lot of in Alaska," he said.

I peered around and pointed to a second one, almost hidden under a fallen branch. "And a few here, apparently. I don't think these are meant for bears, though."

We continued, armed with sticks as we poked our way forward. When we drew closer to the cabin, Morgan stopped us again. Penlight in hand, he waved it along a metal wire running at knee level. We approached with care and bent for a better look.

"Razor wire," I murmured. "Someone really doesn't want visitors."

I decided we'd stick together as we approached the cabin. With this many booby-traps outside, I couldn't send Morgan up there alone. As we drew close, I listened, but heard nothing from the dark building. There was a generator to the side, but it wasn't running.

"Looks like no one's home," Morgan whispered.

I was nodding when I caught a scent. Not a human scent. Something else, something almost as familiar.

Morgan went still and I knew he'd picked it up, too.

I glanced at Clay.

"Yeah, I smell it," he murmured at my shoulder. "Let me have a look."

He took one step around the side of the cabin, then stopped. I hurried over and leaned around to see him standing in front of a darkened window, staring up. A gleaming wolf skull stared back.

Twelve

WE ASCERTAINED THAT the cabin was indeed unoccupied. Then Clay snapped the door lock. It was a simple one—apparently, with all the traps, the owner didn't expect anyone to get close enough to try the door. Clay went in first, looking and listening and sniffing. I waited until he'd checked all through the small cabin and came out to say he was absolutely sure it was empty. Then I stationed Morgan on the porch and slipped inside.

Clay had lit a lantern. I didn't make it past the hall before I stopped. I stood there, gaping into the main room. If the old woman with the nightgown and rifle looked like something from a cartoon, this looked like a set from a horror movie.

Our blond heroine, having miraculously survived chasing a knife-wielding vandal into the forest, soon finds herself lost. She stumbles through the snow until, in the distance, she sees lights. It's a cabin. An unoccupied cabin, to be sure, but she's freezing—being half-naked in a snowstorm can do that do you. So she rushes toward the cabin, finds it unlocked and stumbles in gratefully, then looks up to see…

Dead animals. A whole lotta dead animals, all staring back at me. Some were stuffed and mounted, while others were just pelts, heads attached, glass eyes inserted. That was creepy enough. But in any good horror movie, you need more. You need weapons. Here, they lined every wall—ancient guns, machetes, knives…

Clay stood by the wolf skull. There were actually three of them—one facing out the window, two facing in. All sat atop a wolf pelt.

"That explains the smell," I said, waving at the pelt. "Not a werewolf. Just someone who really likes wolves." I paused and looked around, seeing a few more skulls and pelts. "Dead ones, at least."

While the wolf skulls on the table suggested they deserved a place of honor, the cabin owner was an equal-opportunity predator fan. Every skull and stuffed beast and pelt came from one. I must have subconsciously realized that when I walked in, which is what stopped me in my tracks. It's also what made the room look more like a scene from a horror movie than a simple hunter's retreat. Not a single buck's head or stuffed duck. Instead, I saw coyotes and foxes and bobcats and weasels.

There was even a huge wolverine pelt, right above a polished bear skull. I could smell them all, too, and they were putting my nerves on edge.

I looked over at Clay to comment, but he was absorbed examining something on a shelf. I could make out a white sliver of skull. I walked over and, for the second time, stopped short. There were, again, three skulls on display. All from the same predator.

"Those are..." I began. "I mean, they are, right? They aren't apes..."

"Human," he said.

The outer two were yellowed with age. The middle one was slightly smaller and polished white, like the finger-bones in the cave. I moved closer and lowered my head for a sniff.

"Bleach," I murmured.

Clay nodded. "The others are old. This one isn't." He bent for a closer look. "Can't tell much from a skull, but it looks young and male."

Morgan appeared in the doorway. I waved him in.

"So that skull belongs to the missing kid we found?" he said. "Ricky Rivera?"

"No," Clay said. "We're postulating that it *could* belong to the dead body we found, which *could* be Ricky Rivera."

Morgan looked annoyed, as if Clay was making a petty distinction. He wasn't. If you start making logic leaps like that, you end up in all sorts of trouble. Years of investigating have taught us to keep everything theoretical until we have proof.

I started for the door, planning to take over guard duty on the porch. I'd seen everything I needed to—time to let Morgan satisfy his curiosity while Clay searched for more. As I was leaving, I noticed a low shelf covered in bones.

I bent to examine the bones. Morgan reached over my shoulder for one. I stopped him.

"Paw bones," I said. "They look animal."

"These ones aren't," Clay said.

I turned to see Clay crouched at a bookshelf. It was stuffed with books, but one lower shelf had a gap between the tomes, scattered with small bones.

I walked over to see that they weren't "scattered" at all. They were finger bones, like the ones we'd seen in the cave, arranged in a pattern.

"They're a little bigger than the ones in the cave," Clay said. "Bleached, too, though more recently."

I could smell that. The bleach on the others had been faint, like the skull. This was strong enough to smell from several feet away.

Clay stood, head tilting to read the titles on the books.

"Someone likes anthropology," he said. "Lots of folklore and ritual. Can you snap shots of these, darling? I don't recognize some of the titles."

I took cell phone photos while Morgan watched.

"This guy seems to be our killer," he said. "And we don't smell a werewolf here. Meaning the murderer isn't a man-eater. So this isn't the Pack's responsibility, right?"

"Just because this guy has the bones, doesn't mean he killed anyone," Clay said.

Again, Morgan looked annoyed. "Right, and the blood in the cave?"

"Could be animal."

"Clay's right," I said. "We have lots of pieces here, and it's natural to want to fit them together. But we need more. Are these definitely from those bodies? Is this the murderer or a scavenger? And what about the eating? Animal scavenger? Man-eating werewolf? Cannibal human? Dark magic? Once we eliminate the supernatural possibilities, we're free to go. Until then, we'd better get comfy in Westwood."

WE FINALLY MADE it back to town, coming out on a residential road just north of the main street. As we walked, I kept thinking about what we'd found. I hadn't really before. Sure, that was pretty much all I'd *been* thinking of, but in an abstract way. How did those victims die? Who did it? Why? Now, seeing houses was like a cold slap, waking me up and reminding me that we hadn't just found bodies—we'd found people. Two young men who'd been murdered, their bodies mutilated.

That should be the first thing I think of, shouldn't it? It used to be. No, that's a lie. It never was. There was a time when I'd blame Clay for my lack of empathy. Clearly I'd been around him too long. I'd started seeing things the way he did. But that gives him too much credit. Or perhaps it gives me too little—that I'd be so easily influenced. But I can't blame him. I can't blame being a werewolf. I can't even blame the fact that I've seen so many bodies that I've built up an immunity. That last one plays a factor, of course. Because I *have* changed. It does take me longer these days to pause and recall that I'm dealing with lost lives. But the truth is that I've never been someone who could see a dead body and instantly mourn a life lost. I know people who do, and I feel like I should. But I don't. I do mourn; it just takes longer.

"You okay?" Clay whispered.

"Mmm-hmm. Just thinking."

Morgan cleared his throat. "I don't know about you guys, but I'm freezing. I'm going to kick it up a notch and get back to the motel."

Clay nodded. Morgan murmured for us to call in the morning, and he took off, jogging down the snowy sidewalk. I watched him go. When he reached the corner, I took a deep breath, sucking in cold air to wake myself up.

"Okay, we need a plan for morning," I said. "We've got our booby-trapping, predator-fixated hermit's name on that list, so I can research that. You can look up those books from his cabin. I'll touch base with Paige and Jaime on the symbols." I sighed. "Lots of little pieces, none of them seeming to add up to—"

I stopped, my attention caught by a sign in a yard.

We stood in front of a small two-story house with a car in the drive. Just your typical family home. On the lawn were two signs, one a weathered, "Our Son is a Werewolf!", the other newer and larger, dominated by a huge picture of Ricky Rivera and, "Please Help Bring Our Ricky Home!"

I stared at that sign. Then I wrenched my gaze away and looked at the house. It was dark except for a single second-story light. Was that Ricky's room? The light left on to bring him home?

I took a deep breath. Clay's arm went around me, his warm breath on my cold cheek as he bent to whisper, "It might not have been him."

"It was," I said. "I know we're trying to keep an open mind. But we know that was him and I just keep thinking what if it was..."

"I know."

"I don't think I could handle..."

"I know."

As we stood there, I thought of the playground back home, in Bear Valley. Of what had happened just last week. The weather had been nice—cold but sunny—and I jumped at the chance to take the kids to the playground for some much-needed socializing. Yes, my children's idea of socializing is to be in the same place as other kids, interacting only when physical contact occurs and avoiding that as much as possible. But it's better than total social isolation, which is our natural bent.

At the playground, I'm one of *those* parents. Like hawks watching their fledglings' first flight from the nest, endlessly circling, endlessly hovering. I'm not standing on the sidelines yelling, "Don't go up there! Hold on tight! Watch your step!" But that doesn't mean I'm not thinking it, cringing with every reckless move my little daredevils make.

That day, though, I'd resolved not to hover. On the drive, I'd been encouraging them to join in with other children's games, then I arrived and saw the other mothers huddled on the benches, sipping coffee and chatting, me off to the side, oblivious and alone, and realized I really wasn't setting a good example for the twins. So I took out my thermos, went over and sat with the other parents. I talked, too, letting the conversation engage more and more of my attention until…

Until Kate's scream of pain.

That's when she fell. When I wasn't paying attention. I heard her scream and I leaped up and I saw her there, huddled beside the big slide, Logan shoving past other kids as he raced down the ladder.

They'd been arguing, they later admitted. She wanted to slide down together and he didn't. They tussled. She fell over the side. And I hadn't seen it. I hadn't heard them fighting. I hadn't seen her fall. I hadn't been there to catch her. I'd been preoccupied and she'd been hurt and it could have been so, so much worse.

Back then, when I'd thought it could have been worse, I'd been thinking of the fall, if she'd hit wrong or landed on her back. Now as I looked at Ricky's house, at that single light, I realized just how much worse it could have been. It would have taken no longer than that preoccupied moment for someone to grab her.

I shoved my hands in my pockets. "The world's a dangerous place for kids already. And our corner of it's even worse. Are we being careful enough? Should I even be out here? Should I be Alpha? What if a supernatural did this and tries to retaliate when we catch him? What if some mutt, at any point, tries to retaliate for whatever—"

Clay cut me off, both arms going around me as he stepped in front of me. "No one protects their kids like we do. They have the whole Pack watching out for them. If you stopped chasing guys like this, that wouldn't make anyone less likely to come after our kids. Same as if you decided not to become

Alpha. It would only show that you're afraid. That would make you—and them—a target. You need to do exactly what you are doing—carrying on as if no one would dare touch our children while making sure they're so well-guarded that no one could."

I nodded. He was right, of course. Holing up in my cave with my pups was a sign of fear. Fear was a sign of weakness. Killers—werewolves or not—prey on that.

Clay continued, "I'm sure this boy's parents watched out for him, but they aren't werewolves."

I nodded. I knew he was telling himself that made a difference. Maybe it did. But he said it because he needed to believe it. He's Clayton Danvers and we're the Pack and our children are safe. But the truth was that all it took was one distracted moment in a playground, and they could be gone. Forever.

I looked back at that lit window and let Clay prod me along the sidewalk.

WE REACHED OUR motel room door. Morgan's light was out. Had he gone to bed already?

Clay sighed when he saw me looking in that direction. "Yeah, I'll go check on him."

"Sorry," I said. "It's just…"

"I know."

I opened our door as Clay started walking past. Then he stopped, wheeled and pushed through, shouldering past me. As I regained my balance, he lifted a hand, telling me to stay back. He looked around, eyes narrowing.

"The room is empty," I said. "The door was locked. No one is under the bed…"

"Someone's been in here."

"Yes, restocking the mini-bar, which I'm about to appreciate. Just as soon as *I* go check on Morgan."

Clay was there in a shot, gripping my elbow to stop me.

"Hold on," he said.

Before I could say a word, I caught the intruder's scent. And I noticed a cracked-open drawer with clothing peeking out. A water bottle I'd left on top had been knocked over, water pooled on the floor.

I walked over and inhaled deeper. "It's the same guy who slashed Morgan's tires. Probably ours, too." I motioned at the drawer. "The room's been searched. Better see what's missing."

We started to look. A few minutes later, a knock came at the door. Clay opened it to find Morgan standing there.

"Just got back," he said. "I walked down to the gas station—it's the only place open to grab a pop. I came back to find someone has been in my room. Nothing's missing, but I doubt this place has turndown service. And I don't want to be paranoid, but it smelled like—"

"The vandal we chased earlier today," I said. "Whatever he was looking for, I don't think he found it. My laptop was still hidden. There's nothing else personal in our room."

"I'll help you check yours," Clay said. "Elena?"

"Lock and bolt the door behind you," I said. "Yes, sir."

Morgan

MORGAN GLANCED OVER his shoulder as Clay followed him back to his room. He'd like to take this sudden show of interest as a positive sign—Clayton was worried about him. But he knew better. The guy just didn't trust him to conduct a thorough sniff-search on his own.

Morgan opened the door. Clay walked in, looked around and grunted. It could be approval for Morgan's housekeeping—the room was spotless except for the duffle in the corner. Or he might just have gas.

Clay walked to the duffle, bent and opened it.

Sure, go ahead. Look through that. I don't mind.

Morgan pretended to sniff-search the rest of the room. He'd already done that, but he didn't dare just stand by and let Clay do the work.

"Our intruder rifled through your duffle," Clay said. "Was there anything to find?"

"I know better than that."

"Just checking." Clay rose. "You gonna be okay here tonight?"

Morgan glowered at him. "I am capable of looking after myself. I know I've screwed up but—"

"It was a question, not a jab."

Clay turned to leave.

"Wait," Morgan said.

Clay stopped at the door, one hand on the knob. He turned.

"Look," Morgan said. "I know I stayed out of the fight in Alaska. I know that didn't impress you."

"You're not Pack. I didn't expect you to fight for the Pack."

Yes, but it hadn't just been a fight for the Pack. That was what kept Morgan awake some nights. He'd known about the gang of werewolves. And he hadn't done anything. That's how he'd been raised, but it wasn't an excuse. Even when the Pack showed up, he'd helped, but hadn't joined the fight.

Clay started to leave. Then he stopped, as if considering. He backed inside, closed the door again and turned to Morgan.

"Elena seems to think you might be interested in joining the Pack."

"I…haven't really decided…"

"But you might be. That's why you were coming to Stonehaven, wasn't it? To check things out."

When Morgan didn't answer, annoyance flickered across Clay's face. Morgan didn't blame him really. Obviously that's why he was on their territory, heading to their home. So why couldn't he admit it?

"The Pack needs wolves," Clay said. "Finding them is Elena's job. Pretty soon the whole Pack will be her job."

Morgan blinked, taking a moment to process that. "She's going to be Alpha?"

"Is that a problem?" Clay's voice had dropped to a growl.

"Um, no. I just…" He straightened. "It's not a problem. Just a surprise. But I guess it shouldn't be. I saw how she handled things in Alaska. And now here. She'll make a good leader."

A little too kiss-ass? Maybe. It was hard to tell from Clay's expression, but he didn't exactly light up with pride. Yeah, too kiss-ass. Morgan swallowed. Damn it, why was this so complicated? It was like walking a tightrope, never sure exactly where to find the sweet spot between submission and assertion. That must come naturally to guys who'd grown up in the Pack. Not for him.

Clay took another step into the room, making Morgan inch back. "In five years, she's found two suitable wolves," Clay said. "Reese and Noah. You met them in Alaska. One's in college and one's not even out of high school. They're great kids, but they won't be full Pack members for years. That's all she can get. She's frustrated and discouraged." He took another step. "You want in? You step up. Don't toy with her. Understood?"

Morgan nodded. "Understood."

Thirteen

I WAS IN BED, on my laptop looking up our predator-obsessed cabin dweller when Clay came back. He didn't say anything, just went into the bathroom, then came out, undressed and crawled into bed, being careful not to disturb me.

An hour later, when I stretched, I was sure he'd fallen asleep. But he opened one eye and said, "Find anything?"

I shook my head. "No. I think that's why we call them hermits. We know he's not a mutt. We can't find out if he's in the council records until morning, and even then, I doubt this"—I pointed at the list—"is his real name if he's a supernatural. Hell, it probably isn't his real name either way, so how am I going to…" I shook my head. "I'm too tired. Just getting frustrated."

Clay pulled me against him. "We're gonna find whoever did this. Supernatural or not. Then we'll make sure the kid's parents know. Give them some closure."

I reached up to kiss his cheek. "Thank you."

He tugged me on top of him, one arm around my waist, the other hand on the back of my head, pulling me down into a kiss. "Now, let's see about helping you get a good night's sleep."

The problem with small-town motels? Lack of room service. It's not usually a huge issue. I've always balked at paying the insane prices anyway, so I normally roll out of bed and hunt down breakfast myself. But this particular small town wasn't exactly bulging with dining options. The motel didn't even have vending machines, as Morgan had discovered last night. So Clay and I were dressed within minutes of waking, and heading out the door about sixty seconds later.

We'd been up until almost dawn, so it was past ten. That meant our ride—scheduled for service at eight—should be done. Except, as we jogged along the main street, we could see the SUV ahead, still buried in snow.

"That doesn't look ready to drive," I said.

"No," Clay growled. "It does not."

I kept going, just in case the mechanic had miraculously managed to change our tires while not disturbing its snow blanket. He hadn't, of course. There weren't even boot prints in the surrounding snow to suggest someone had taken a look.

I called the garage. It took a while for someone to answer. When a woman did, I explained the problem.

"We really do need to get home," I said. "We have small children and this wasn't supposed to be an overnight trip. What time is the mechanic coming?"

"You need to make an appointment." The receptionist sounded bored, TV blasting in the background.

"I did, as I explained. For eight this morning. He said we didn't need to be here—he'd change the tires and bill us. Is he running behind?"

"If he is, he hasn't told me. But *that's* not your problem. Your problem is that you canceled the appointment."

"What?"

She spoke slower, as if to someone of limited intelligence. "You called this morning and said you didn't need service."

"If I did, I would remember it, wouldn't I?" I bit my tongue and softened my tone. "Okay, clearly there's been a mixup, so—"

"No mixup. You called. Elena Michaels, just like on the work order. You said you didn't need service."

"And I spoke to you? Did it sound like me?"

A pause. I knew it hadn't—my Canadian accent doesn't stand out nearly as much around here as Clay's southern drawl, but it was distinctive enough.

"I don't pay no mind," the woman said finally. "Woman calls, says she's Elena Michaels, getting her tires fixed this morning, that's good enough for me."

"All right then. When can I reschedule for?"

A deep sigh, then a creak, as if I'd made her get out of her chair. A moment later, paper shuffled. "Same time tomorrow."

"What? No. Look, I understand there was a mistake, and it's not your fault, but I have children at home and I need to get back today."

"Then you shouldn't have canceled the appointment."

Clay, who'd been listening in, held out his hand. I hesitated. Then I decided she deserved it—and I really did want to get home—so I handed over the phone.

Clay went easy on her. He had to—there was little to stop her from hanging up and stranding us here. But even his "easy" is, admittedly, more effective than my worst. He managed to get her to agree to have someone out before nightfall. That was the best we could do. So we continued toward the diner on foot.

"I'll call Jeremy," I said. "He might be able to get someone sooner. If not, at least he can be ready to pick us up for the night himself. It's not like we're stuck in the middle of nowhere." I looked around at the empty, snow-filled streets. "It just feels like it."

"I know. We'll get home tonight. Even if we don't, the kids will survive."

I nodded. Just yesterday, I couldn't get out of the house fast enough. That seemed to be the way it went. We'd go stir-crazy if we were home too long, but it didn't take much time away before we wanted to go back.

"The dispatcher didn't seem too bright," I said. "Do you think she just screwed up? Or did someone call and cancel our appointment?"

"Hard to say. But if a woman called, there's only one woman who knew we were getting our car serviced this morning."

"Chief Dales."

"Yep."

I glanced over my shoulder at the police station.

"Food first," Clay said. "I'm too hungry to stand back and watch you be diplomatic."

"And I'm too hungry to be diplomatic. Food it is, then."

Morgan

MORGAN ROLLED OVER and looked at the clock. It was after ten. No wonder he was so hungry. He stretched and yawned. As he did, he noticed a white piece of paper under the door. The bill?

He padded over and picked it up. It was a handwritten note.

Checking car, then going to diner for breakfast. Join us when you're up.

Ten minutes later, Morgan was still in his shorts, sitting on the edge of the bed, staring at the note. Elena wanted him in the Pack. No, that was overstating it—she wanted him to put his name forward so he could be evaluated for Pack membership. The "evaluated" part didn't bother him. It was like any other club—if it'll take just anyone, there's a catch. Of course, one always hoped that, having made your acquaintance, they'd be happy to have you, no admission tests required. But if Elena offered him membership based on their short acquaintance, he'd be suspicious. He should be flattered they were even offering to consider him.

He *was* flattered. Maybe even a little surprised. That's where the problem lay. The Pack offered brotherhood and protection, which he wanted. But it was a reciprocal relationship. You got the brotherhood and the protection because everyone joined in to provide it. You couldn't take without giving back.

So what did he have to give? Most werewolves couldn't join a real wolf pack for almost two years as he had. The social isolation would drive them mad. Morgan had missed the human world, but not enough to quit his experiment. That was a good clue that he wasn't the most sociable guy. If he did join the Pack, how often would he excuse himself from the meetings and other gatherings? Not often—he did want that brotherhood. But there would be times when he just wasn't in the mood to offer it back.

The bigger problem was the second part of the equation. Protection. The Pack needed fighters and Morgan was not a fighter. Not by any stretch of the imagination. He'd gone to a rough-and-tumble rural school, but managed to avoid brawls, namely because he was so damned average. He wasn't smart enough or different enough to be bullied. He wasn't big enough or athletic enough to be challenged. He'd been raised to stay under the radar. Be invisible. Avoid confrontation. He couldn't afford to risk revealing his enhanced strength. So he could count on one hand the number of brawls he'd gotten into, and he'd lost every one, because he hadn't stuck around to finish the fight.

Elena wouldn't expect him to be in prime fighting condition. She'd anticipate that training would be required. So would Clay—Morgan doubted any recruit would meet his standards. But when Clay found out they'd have to begin at square one, with "how to throw a punch without breaking your fingers"? Morgan didn't even want to think how he'd react. He wouldn't laugh. That wasn't his style. But Morgan would sink so low in his regard that he'd never climb back out again.

Clay was right. If Morgan wasn't sure he wanted to join the Pack, then he was messing with Elena. She didn't need that. And Morgan didn't need to piss off Clayton Danvers. They'd already been pulled into this mess because of him. He should back out while he could.

He got up and dressed, then wrote a note of his own and put it under Elena's door.

SO *NOW WHAT?* Morgan thought as he headed along the sidewalk, hunched against the cold. Walk to the highway and hitch a ride to…? To where? Back to Alaska? To Newfoundland? No, there was nothing for him there.

He stopped and looked around. What the hell was he doing? He'd driven nearly a week to get to the Pack and now he was having second thoughts? No, not having second thoughts. Chickening out. Running away.

Maybe he didn't think he was Pack material, but wasn't that up to the Pack to decide? There wasn't any penalty for trying. Elena had told him that in Alaska. He could go to Stonehaven, hang out with them for a weekend, and if he wasn't interested, that was fine. If he did apply and was rejected, he'd be no worse off than he was now. They weren't going to chase him to the state border and vow to kill him if they ever saw him again. It would be an amicable parting. Elena would see to that.

He would tell Clay upfront about the fighting issue. No, he'd tell Elena. That felt a little cowardly, but it also seemed safest. He could explain the situation to her, and she could warn Clayton. They might count it as a strike against his membership, but at least Morgan would have been honest about it.

Before he realized he was even walking again, he found himself back in the motel parking lot.

I made a bad impression, he thought, *but I can fix it. I will fix it. Just—*

He stopped as a scent wafted past. Turning, he saw a teenage boy sliding a keycard into Morgan's motel room door. He was wearing a parka, but the hood was down, showing his face. Morgan didn't recognize that face, but he did know the parka—and the scent. It was the vandal who'd slashed his tires.

The kid turned, as if sensing Morgan there. Morgan leaped forward. The kid bolted. Morgan tossed his duffel into the bushes and he tore after him.

Fourteen

WE'D SETTLED IN for breakfast at the diner. Pancakes were on the menu, so that's what I ordered. We got biscuits too, just to have something to keep our stomachs from growling while we waited for the meal. I'd already had two—and a cup of coffee—and was trying not to eye the kitchen impatiently.

"You know," I said. "I'm getting that feeling of being watched again."

"Huh." Clay ripped apart his fourth biscuit. "Don't know why."

The diner was nearly full, and I swore every one of those patrons—plus the server and even the cook—had found an excuse to walk past our table. At least half of them were gaping at us.

"This is why I hate small towns," Clay muttered.

"You also hate small cities. And big ones. The common factor? They all contain people." I glanced around. "We should take advantage of our popularity. Ask about our hermit guy. But we need to be discreet. Subtly follow someone out—"

Clay turned his chair so fast it squeaked, startling the guy behind us, who'd been leaning in to eavesdrop.

"Hey," Clay said. "We were hiking yesterday and nearly lost a leg in a bear trap near a cabin. You know anything about that?"

The guy yanked in his chair fast. "Nope."

Clay turned to the woman on his other side, who'd been doing her share of gaping—though only at him. "How about you?"

"N-no." She dropped her gaze, blushing furiously, as if she'd been caught cheating on her husband. "Sorry."

Our breakfast arrived as I was glaring at Clay.

"Hey," he said to the server. "Got a question—"

I kicked him under the table. He shot me a look, then turned back to her as she set out the food.

"Were you the one who served our friend the other night?" Clay said. "The guy whose car is stuck in your parking lot?"

"Uh-huh," she said, laying out the plates.

Now the man behind Clay perked up again. "Oh, is that the one who was running around naked in the woods?" He laughed. "You better tell your friend he needs to learn to hold his liquor better." He poked the server. "And you need to learn when to stop serving drunk guys, Marnie. Even if they are handsome young men."

I looked up at the server. "He was drinking?"

She swallowed, then said, casually, "Uh-huh. He seemed fine, so I kept serving. It was only a few whiskeys, but I guess he can't hold his liquor very well."

She was lying. Even if I couldn't tell that from her gaze, I would have smelled liquor on Morgan yesterday morning. I hadn't. He'd said he didn't have a drink and nothing about his scent had claimed otherwise.

I glanced at Clay. He was already attacking breakfast. The server backed away, then scampered off.

"She's lying," I said.

"Yep."

"Why?"

"No idea." He waved at my plate. "Eat up. We need to leave so someone can follow us out."

"What?"

"Just eat."

WE LEFT THE diner. I was about to begin the long walk back to our motel, but Clay waved me over to Morgan's disabled car, now a snowdrift in the lot.

"What are we—?" I began.

"Stalling."

"Because..."

"Someone will talk to us. Just not in there."

I should have known that. I'd learned long ago that some people, particularly in small communities, are happy to gossip with strangers...just not in front of their neighbors. That's what Clay had been doing when he'd asked about the traps. He didn't expect an answer from the people he singled out. He was just setting the stage. I've pulled similar ploys, though a little more discreetly. The fact that I didn't realize what he was doing proved just how little sleep I'd gotten, my dreams haunted by missing children.

Sure enough, as we were clearing off Morgan's car with our hands, a family came out and headed our way. The couple was around our age. Regular-looking folks, a dark-haired man and his red-headed wife. They had two kids with them. The woman leaned over and whispered something and the kids took off for the family's car.

"You're going to need a snow brush for that," the man called as they approached.

"Or a shovel," I said with a smile.

"I can help with the brush," he said. "Let me go grab mine."

And with that, *he* set the stage, giving them an excuse to chat with the strangers, should anyone be watching. While he headed off to retrieve the brush, his wife introduced herself.

"Michelle Woodvine," she said. "I heard about the traps. I'm so sorry. I've said before that there should be warning signs. Everyone in town knows they're there, but visitors don't."

"We saw them, luckily," I said. "Do you guys actually get bears around here?"

She sighed. "No. It's just… It's Charlie. A local man who's…having some problems. Psychological problems. Everyone remembers how he used to be, though, so no one wants to make a big deal. Like he'll just wake up one morning and snap out of it."

"Charlie?"

"Lacoste," Michelle said, though I already knew the name from my research. "He grew up here in Westwood. Headed off to college in New York, then went backpacking and didn't come home for nearly twenty years."

Her husband came back and handed Clay the brush, letting him clean while we chatted.

"Charlie got wrapped up in all kinds of crazy stuff out there," the husband said. "Witchcraft in Africa. Voodoo in the Caribbean. Mysticism in the East. Then he came back. Married a local woman with a little boy. Taught history at the high school. Just a regular guy again."

"Until his wife died," Michelle said. "He got in a big fight with his son. And he started…losing it. Living in the woods, setting traps, scaring off anyone who came by."

"Sounds dangerous."

The three of us stood there, the silence broken only by the *swish-swish* of the snow brush as Clay cleared. They knew I was thinking of the body we'd found. I could tell by their expressions—almost guilty, as if they'd played some role by not pushing harder to get help for Charlie Lacoste.

Finally, Michelle said, "If he killed that young drifter, it wasn't intentional. We were thinking about that earlier. Maybe the young man wandered onto his property, got hurt, then wandered off again. Bled to death or died of exposure."

Which still made Charlie Lacoste guilty. But I didn't say that.

"I'm sure Jess would have already brought Charlie in for questioning if she could," the husband said. "But he went missing about a couple months back. No one's seen him. Not even his son."

"His son's in Westwood?" I said.

They nodded in unison. Then Michelle said, "His name's Hanlon. Pete Hanlon. He kept his dad's name when his mother married Charlie."

"Pete Hanlon. The football coach?"

Another simultaneous nod. With that we had our morning planned out. A visit to Chief Dales, followed by one to Coach Hanlon, to talk about his stepdad.

Morgan

THE KID WHO'D slashed Morgan's tires apparently wasn't keen on getting caught. Still, it wasn't exactly a fast chase—the sidewalks were covered in snow. In fact, as Morgan slid and stumbled after him, it probably looked pretty damned ridiculous. Like a chase scene shot in slow motion. The kid fell once, which might have helped, if Morgan hadn't fallen twice. He was accustomed to running through deep snow in wolf form. As a human? Not so much.

The kid kept glancing back, his expression growing darker each time, as if to say "Are you still there? Give up already, dude." But Morgan was nothing if not tenacious. At least, he could be, when he wasn't backing down and running away.

Finally they were heading into the commercial heart of Westwood. The sidewalks were shoveled here and people were out and about, shopping and socializing in the wake of yesterday's storm. The kid wisely decided running down a busy street might not be his best option. He ducked between two shops. Morgan chased him along the narrow alley. The kid veered behind the shop…and went flying as his boots slid in snow-dusted mud.

Morgan tackled the boy, grabbed him by the front of his parka and put him up against the wall. The kid struggled. He struggled quite well, actually, suggesting there was an athletic build under that bulky parka. Not that it did any good. Morgan might not be a fighter, but he was a werewolf, with a werewolf's strength. He held him easily. As the boy fought, Morgan took a better look at him. Acne-pocked cheeks. Short dark hair. Sullen expression. Maybe sixteen, even seventeen.

"Who told you to slash my tires?" Morgan said.

"No one. I don't like strangers."

"So you just slashed my tires and my friends' for kicks? And broke into our motel rooms for fun?"

The kid hadn't denied that he was the vandal. He didn't deny this either—didn't even seem to pause to wonder how Morgan knew. Clearly not someone with a lot of criminal experience. Or a lot of brains.

"I was looking for money. You city folks always have money."

"You left fifty bucks in my bag. My mini-bar wasn't even opened. You were looking for something specific. And someone gave you keycards to find it."

Now the kid started thinking. And looking worried. "I-I don't know what you're talking about."

"My door wasn't broken. My friends' door wasn't broken. Those motel doors close and lock automatically, meaning whoever came in used a keycard, which he could only get from someone who worked there. Do you work there?"

The kid shook his head.

"Then someone who does gave you those cards, and is probably the same someone who told you to break in, and told you what to look for."

"N-no. I found your card. It was..." He looked around. "In the snow. You must have dropped it."

"And my friends dropped theirs, but both magically reappeared in our pockets later." Morgan shook his head. "How about you tell that story to my friends. See what they think of it."

Morgan flipped the kid around and grabbed the back of his jacket. "Walk."

The kid took two stumbling steps, as if trying to figure out his next move. Morgan was giving him a helpful shove when a figure walked out from the alley.

"Thought I heard voices," the man said. "What's going on here?"

Another man joined him. Both were about Morgan's age, burly. One wore an old Werewolves football jacket. They bore down on Morgan, coming close enough for him to smell last night's beer on their breath.

"You like little boys?" asked the guy in the team jacket.

"Only ones who slash my tires and break into my motel room."

The guy walked past the kid, gripped in Morgan's hand. He leaned right into Morgan's face. "You made a mistake."

"Um, no, I—"

"Yeah, you did. Now let him go."

Morgan paused. "All right. I will. At the police station. They can settle this. If he didn't do it, I'll even apologize for the inconvenience."

A third guy had appeared. Middle-aged. Hanging back, watching, uncertain. When Morgan tried to nudge the kid forward, the young guy in the team jacket grabbed the boy and thrust him toward the older man.

"Bill? Take Jason home. Clive and I will handle this."

"Handle what?" Morgan said, voice rising as Bill led the boy around the corner. "I didn't hurt the kid. I chased him and cornered him and now I want to take him to the police station to straighten this out. You can escort us there if you'd like."

The guy in the team jacket took a swing. Morgan saw it coming and ducked. He backed up.

"Look, maybe you don't like outsiders accusing town kids of committing crimes, but this isn't the way to handle—"

The other guy—Clive—swung. Morgan managed to dodge again, only to come up straight into Team Jacket's fist. Apparently, no one else was interested in handling this properly. Not when the alternative gave these two thugs a chance to beat the crap out of a stranger.

Morgan fought back. He could manage that—he wasn't completely inept. And he had the advantage of strength, so it wasn't nearly as humiliating as it would be against a couple of werewolves. He managed to land a hard right to the side of Clive's head. The guy dropped. Team Jacket charged. Morgan grabbed him by the coat, threw him aside and raced for the alley.

He rounded the corner to find himself facing a small mob headed by a middle-aged Latino woman.

"What did you do to my boy?" she demanded.

"Boy?" He looked toward the street. The guy with the kid was gone. "If that was your son, I apologize for chasing him, but he broke into—"

"That wasn't her son," one of the men snapped. "She's Ricky's mom."

Ricky? Shit. The missing kid. Ricky Rivera.

Morgan backed up, hands lifted. "I didn't do anything to anyone. I just got here the night before last. I—"

Team Jacket charged Morgan. He stepped aside and the guy went flying. As Morgan turned, someone in the mob took a swing. An awkward swing, from someone even less accustomed to fighting than him. He managed to catch the guy's arm and throw him down. Then he wheeled to find Mrs. Rivera in his path again.

"Are you going to attack me, too?" she asked.

"I haven't attacked anyone," he said, struggling to keep the snarl from his voice. "I've defended myself against a bunch of—" He swallowed the last words. Insulting the locals really wouldn't help. "Just take me to the police station and I'll explain—"

Two men jumped Morgan from behind. He went down, face first in the muddy snow, his attackers piling onto his back.

"You'll explain now," Mrs. Rivera said. "I don't trust that lady cop—"

"This isn't the way you folks want to handle this," said a distant voice, growing closer. "Whatever you think of Jess Dales, Maria, she's the chief of police here. I'm going to take this man to the station and let them handle it."

The mob parted. A hand reached down to help Morgan up. He took it.

Fifteen

WE WERE WALKING away from the diner when a police cruiser pulled into the lot. We waited by the front walk as Officer Kent got out.

"Fueling up before tackling that list the chief gave you?" I said as he approached.

"List?"

"Guys living off the grid around here. I heard her mention it last night when we stopped by the station. She said you and Officer Jaggerman were handling it this morning."

We stepped aside for an elderly couple exiting the diner.

"Right," Kent said. "No. She changed her mind. Has me running errands today."

We said goodbye and headed for the road.

"So, is that coincidence?" I said. "Chief Dales just happened to leave that list for us, then decided not to follow up on it? And a woman just happened to cancel the car service that could have let us leave Westwood this morning?"

"She's getting free help," Clay said.

I glanced over.

"I bet she's found out you're a journalist," he said. "You've covered missing persons cases in Canada. Maybe you'd like to do a little investigative reporting as long as you're stuck here. Doesn't seem like the local cops are exactly homicide experts."

"But she runs the risk that I *will* write an article, and that it won't exactly be complimentary to the Westwood PD."

He shrugged. "If she's done her research, she knows you're not a muckraker. Maybe she's hoping negative publicity would boost the budget. Get her some decent cops. Or maybe she's just making a very stupid mistake. She's young."

"Either way, we should have that chat with her. Coach Hanlon can wait."

❧

WE ARRIVED AT the station to find Officer Jaggerman behind the counter.

"Chief's out on the case," he said.

"Do you know when she'll—?" I began.

The night officer, apparently putting in more overtime, walked in from the back room, cordless phone in hand. He walked over to Jaggerman.

"Just got a call," he said. "Seems there's a disturbance over behind the old feed store."

"Disturbance?" Jaggerman said.

"Couple guys going at it."

Jaggerman snorted and waved him off. "Cabin fever. Let 'em duke it out."

He turned back to me. "No, I don't know when she'll be back. I tried her cell a few minutes ago and she wasn't answering. When she calls, I'll let her know you're looking for her."

I thanked him and we left.

CLAY AND I returned to the motel. I'd left a note for Morgan to join us for breakfast, and hoped he hadn't headed there while we were in the station. It looked like he might have—he didn't answer when I rapped on his door.

"Could be sleeping," Clay said. "You know what Noah and Reese are like. If they don't have school, they sleep until noon, and it takes a bullhorn to wake them up."

Morgan was older than the boys and likely past that stage, but I didn't say so. Clay would just snort that he acted that age. He didn't. But, sadly, you reach that point in life where anyone under the age of thirty is a kid.

We went to the motel office. The clerk—an elderly man—sat behind the desk reading the newspaper. I approached as Clay hung back.

"Our friend in room six isn't answering his door. Could you ring his room for me?"

The clerk didn't look up from is paper. "He checked out."

I frowned. "Are you sure? He's—"

"Young guy? Long hair? Indian?"

Close enough, I supposed, given that the old guy's glasses were on his desktop instead of his nose. I thanked him and we headed for our room. When Clay opened the door, I saw the note shoved under it.

I'd better be moving on. Sorry for any trouble I caused. Thanks for helping me out. I owe you.

Clay read the note over my shoulder, then he walked down the sidewalk to Morgan's room. He snapped the lock and opened the door.

I walked into the empty room, looking and sniffing.

"No scent except his," I murmured. "Same for the note. It smells like him. No one else." I paused. "He's gone then."

"I'm sorry, darling."

I nodded, wadded the note and pitched it into the trash.

WE'D HAD NO luck tracking down Chief Dales. Or Coach Hanlon. It was late afternoon. It'd be dark soon, so we decided to hike back to the cabin for more answers. We were close enough to see it when we noticed footprints coming from the forest, deep ones, quickly filling with new snow.

"Someone else headed this way not too long ago," I said as I crouched beside a print. "Small prints made with heavy boots. A kid?"

"Any scent?" Clay asked.

I shook my head. "Too much snow."

"Follow the trail then."

A few feet farther, we found a sprung bear trap, tracks leading up it, then moving past. Looking closer, I saw holes in the snow by each footstep. Someone poking a walking stick into the snow. Someone who knew about the traps.

We'd almost reached the cabin when Clay stopped, head tilted. "Hear that?"

It took a second, then I caught a voice on the breeze.

"Someone talking?" I said.

"Sounds more like chanting."

The sound came from the other side of the cabin. We crept to the building, then paused. Definitely chanting. Not in English either.

I snuck along the side of the cabin, then peered around it to see a circle cleared in the snow. Candles burned at each of the compass points. A woman knelt in the ritual circle, her back to us. Her hood was down, dark hair spilling out over her navy parka.

"Looks like we found Chief Dales," Clay whispered.

"And we found our witch."

Sixteen

IF THERE ARE commandments for Alphas, the first would be "Thou shalt be decisive." When I'd first been bitten—and for years afterwards—I'd mistaken Jeremy's decisiveness for narrow-mindedness. He never seemed to weigh options. He never even seemed to *see* options. When presented with a problem, he'd tell us how to handle it and that was that, as if there was only one possible solution. That wasn't true at all. If Jeremy and I have anything in common, it is that we see too many solutions. There is no black and white for us. We see every way that a situation could be handled, and agonize over the decision, knowing none will be perfect.

The trick, as Alpha, is to *act* otherwise. No one in your Pack wants to see their leader waffling. To follow the Alpha's commands wholeheartedly, they must believe those commands. Kind of like a cult, if you think about it, but when

I jokingly mentioned that to Clay once, I got an hour-long lecture on cult dynamics versus pack mentality. He was right, though I never ceded the point. Werewolves don't obey because we're brainwashed into thinking our leader is all-powerful—we obey because the wolf in us is most comfortable following a leader.

So now I needed to decide what to do about our spell-casting chief of police and the answer was far from simple. I knew what Clay would do—march out there and confront her. Which is why, as he'd be the first to admit, he'd make a lousy Alpha. The problem is that, sometimes, I wish I had a little more of that decisiveness. Instead, I stood behind the cabin, shivering in the cold, as I replayed everything we'd discovered, all our interactions with Chief Dales and what they could mean, in light of our new discovery.

Then I texted Paige. I sent her the chief's name and a photo, and asked if she had any record of her. The Coven records aren't nearly as good as the Pack's dossiers. I could take some pride in that—I've been in charge of the dossiers for almost twenty years. But I only need to track a few dozen werewolves, not hundreds of witches. And, let's be honest, on a per capita basis, my guys are a whole lot more likely to get into the kind of trouble where I need to track them down, fast. It took Paige only a few minutes to report that there wasn't a Jessica Dales in her database, which only meant Dales hadn't been caught causing trouble before. There were a couple families of witches in the area, but most non-Coven ones had forgone their matrilineal system, meaning surnames were often useless. There had not, however, been any reported cases of witches practicing rituals requiring human sacrifice in upstate New York. Which, again, might only mean they hadn't been caught.

As I weighed that, Dales started packing up. That gave me about two minutes to decide—confront her or not. I walked around to the back of the cabin.

"Hey, Jess," I said. "Can I call you that? Jess?"

She jumped. "Oh, Ms. Michaels. I didn't hear—"

"You don't need to do that out here," I said, pointing at the almost obliterated circle. "You can, if it helps for mental preparation, but that whole at-one-with-nature thing is just window dressing. You can perform witch rituals anywhere. I have a friend who can help you with that. Paige Winterbourne? Maybe you've heard of her. Her mother led the American coven. Now Paige is with the interracial council. You know them?"

As I chattered, I watched her expression. One, for signs she had no idea what I was talking about. Two, for signs that she was shocked that *I* was talking about it. When I saw neither, it answered a whole lot of questions. Once I finished, she did rouse herself to proper denials, of course. But I cut her short.

"I know you're a witch," I said. "What concerns me more is that I just started talking about Paige and covens and councils, and you aren't wondering how the hell I know all that."

"Which means you know what *we* are," Clay said.

He'd stepped out behind her. When he spoke, she wheeled. It wasn't until seeing him, though, that she stepped back. She stopped herself, but that reaction erased any doubts.

"You've known since you called me, haven't you?" I said. "You figured out what Morgan was, and when you found my name on his map, you called me to come and take care of it. Get him off your turf. Fast."

"I-I don't—" She cleared her throat and came back stronger. "I don't know what you're talking about. Covens? Councils? Witches? I was waiting for the punch line."

"So you don't know what we are?"

"Besides crazy?"

I took a step toward her. She struggled not to shrink back.

"That's fine," I said. "If you *did* know and you admitted it, we could work something out. I'm all for coexisting. But when people know what we are and pretend they don't, that's a problem. And we're very good at taking care of our problems. Which you'd know, if you knew what we are."

A pause, one so long I swore an inch of snow fell before she answered. "Let's talk."

"Good. We'll go inside."

She shook her head. "It's not my place. I just come here now that Charlie's gone. With all the traps, I know no one will bother me."

"We can open the door. As you said, he's not here."

She hesitated.

"Which would be illegal," I said. "Trespassing. Break and enter. That's not what you're thinking, though. You're a little more concerned about what we'll see inside. All those predators. Especially the wolves. Someone really likes wolves."

"That's Charlie, and it's completely unconnected to..." She glanced at us, then nodded. "Let's go inside." She paused. "And it's Jess. You can call me Jess."

"YES, I KNOW what you are," Jess said as we entered the cabin. "And who you are. I didn't make the connection when I called you because everyone says the stories about your...group living near here are just rumors. Obviously not. I figured it out when you guys showed up, which also explained the issue with your friend. After that, I just wanted you to get the hell out of town. No offense."

"None taken." I took a seat in Charlie's living room. "I can see why you'd want us gone, preferably before we found the dead bodies. Sadly, that didn't quite work out."

She stared at me. "What? You think—? Shit! Of course you do." She paced to the window, struggling to control her breathing, then turned. "I have nothing to do with that body. Witches don't sacrifice people. I thought you'd know that."

"They do for protection rituals," I said. "A high level protection ritual requires a life given for a life protected."

"I protect myself with this." She opened her parka to show her gun. "And I protect my town with this." She gestured at her badge. "That body you found was partially eaten. And not by scavengers. Doc said he found human teeth marks on the bones. That made me think it might be one of yours. We've also had drifters go missing, which could mean we have one of you guys living out here. I know your…group is supposed to handle problems like that, which is why I called you to the station last night and left you that list."

"And stopped us from leaving today?"

"What?"

"A woman called and canceled our car repair this morning."

"That wasn't me," she said.

"You're the only one who knew."

"No, lots of people knew. They saw the car. They asked us if you guys were okay. We said Jim was swinging by this morning to fix it."

"So someone slashed our tires to strand us here, then canceled our repair to keep us here?"

She finally came into the room and took a seat across from me. "I presumed the tire slashing was just kids. We have a few idiots." She paused. "More than a few. It's a small town. They get bored easily. They know better than to lash out at locals, but strangers are fair game. I don't understand the mechanic call, though." She looked around. "And where's your friend?"

"He left."

She frowned. "How? I saw his car at the diner this morning. It wasn't going anywhere."

"Hitch-hiked to the highway, I guess. Morgan's not one of ours. Just coming out to see us and, apparently, after everything that happened, decided to push on instead. But speaking of the diner, did the server tell you Morgan was drunk the other night?"

"Sure. Marnie said he had three, four whiskeys with dinner."

"Did you test him?"

She shook her head. "I couldn't charge the guy with public drunkenness after all that time."

"He wasn't drunk. Didn't have a single drink, he said, and if he did, we'd have smelled it on him the next morning. Your server lied."

"Why?"

"Answering that is your job, isn't it?" Clay drawled.

She looked at him, seemed to consider responding, then decided I was the safer conversationalist and turned her attention back to me.

"Also, if your coroner found human teeth marks on that body, it wasn't one of us," I said. "You'd have found teeth marks like those." I gestured at a wolf skull on the shelf. "Which means you have the kind of problem we can't help you with. And..." I rose and walked to the shelf with the three human skulls on it. "This middle one? It's new. It's been boiled so I don't think you'll get DNA off it, but it's a pretty sure bet that it belongs to Ricky Rivera."

"What?" She scrambled up and stared at the skull. She looked ill and I cursed myself for being so flippant. She'd known Ricky. She'd doubtless come to know him even better in the months she'd been searching for him.

"I'm sorry," I said.

She tore her attention from the middle skull and her gaze tripped over the whole trio. "No. That's not...Charlie wouldn't have...There's no way you can tell that from a skull."

"We found the rest of the body. Minus a skull. Also minus a hand, like our dead drifter. There are some finger bones there." I pointed at the bookcase. "We found more in a cave. We'll show you that, too. Before we do, though, tell us about Charlie."

Seventeen

JESS'S STORY STARTED the same as the couple's from the diner. Town legend, dating back before her time, about the young man who'd gone off to see the world, then came back, took a wife and settled down. Whereas the couple said he'd been just a normal guy until his wife's death, Jess told another version.

"I think people forget," she said. "Or they rework the past to make a better story. I arrived shortly before his wife died, and he was already a little off. According to everyone I talked to, he'd always been that way."

"Off?"

"Eccentric, I should say. Not dangerous. Not ever..." She looked back at the skull, then away. "Some of this was here even before Susan died. Certainly the books. That's what he did abroad. He taught English to make a living, but his real passion was for traveling and gathering stories. Folklore. Myth. Whatever you call it."

"Ritualistic magic," Clay said.

Again, she looked over, as if surprised to hear him speak, and again she hesitated, as if she realized she should include him in the conversation, before turning back to me.

"Yes, ritualistic magic. From all over the world. That's what drew me to him when I moved here. I heard a few things and I wondered if he was a supernatural. So I asked about his interests. Just questions, not interrogation. We became friends, I think. Of a sort. No one else was interested in his hobby, not even his wife and stepson. No one around here seemed to understand. It was just…"

"Weird," I said.

She nodded. "But it was purely an academic interest. He collected some of this, but he didn't do anything with it. He didn't try the rituals. He just learned about them. Until Susan passed away."

"His wife," I said. "And how did she die?"

"Cancer. No possible foul play there. It was quick. Three months and she was gone. But during those three months…" She waved around. "That's when it went from books and memorabilia to all this. The skulls, the skins. He became obsessed with animals."

"Predators."

She blinked, as if she hadn't seen the connection. After a look across the room, she nodded. "Yes, predators, I guess."

"And the traps?"

"That came later. After the fight with his stepson."

"Coach Hanlon."

"Right. Don't ask me what it was about. No one knew. Just a big blowout that pushed Charlie completely off the rails. That's when he started living out here permanently, set up the traps and told the rest of the world to go to hell. Even me."

WE PREPARED TO leave the cabin after that—all of us. I could ask more about Charlie's disappearance. I could tell her about the ritualistic markings we'd seen in the forest. For now, though, we'd shared enough. Time to slow down and process.

What did I think happened? That our eccentric recluse had tipped over into raving madman. The missing drifters dated back to shortly after Charlie's wife died. Shortly after a guy obsessed with ritual and predators started going "off the rails." Now he'd disappeared and we were finding bodies with human teeth marks.

Charlie Lacoste was out here. I was sure of that. He was probably even coming home occasionally to add to his collection. He might be living in the cave, the smoke covering his scent. He had, I believed, become his obsession. Become a predator. A wild beast living in the forest, feeding on whatever he could catch. Including Ricky Rivera.

The sun was setting. We were on the cabin steps when Jess got a call. She looked at her cell phone and winced.

"Mrs. Rivera," she said. "Always fun." With a deep breath, she answered.

I don't know if she realized we had super-hearing—her knowledge of werewolves seemed to be a little scattered—but she retreated into the cabin to talk. I caught a few words. Something about a man who'd been arrested, and there might be a connection to her son's disappearance. Mrs. Rivera was calling to demand more information. Jess seemed to have no idea what she was talking about. A moment later, she came out.

"Well, it seems your friend Morgan didn't take off after all," she said. "According to Mrs. Rivera, he was caught going after one of our teens."

"What?" I said. "No. He wouldn't..." I glanced at Clay. "Our tire-slasher. I bet he spotted the kid when he was leaving town." I turned back to Jess. "Clay and Morgan chased our vandal yesterday and lost him in the woods. Morgan must have seen him again and gone after him."

"I figured it was something like that. I tried to tell her yesterday that he couldn't have taken Ricky. He just got here, and her son disappeared over a year ago. It seems she's convinced that he took him and came back. Now they think he was trying to strike again. Because, if you're going to grab teenage boys, this is the only town that has them." She rolled her eyes.

"So what happened?" I asked.

"A flash mob," she said. "And not the sort that breaks out in song. I don't think they'd have done anything, but luckily, it never came to that. The voice of reason appeared, in the form of our football coach, who has more than his share of experience mediating when testosterone surges. Mrs. Rivera said he took Morgan to the station. We'll get this straightened out. But you really need to keep your friend on a tighter leash." She glanced sharply at Clay. "No pun intended."

He only grunted.

"I'll phone the station and see what's going on."

She didn't bother retreating for this call, and I realized she only had earlier for confidentiality. This was just business. Jaggerman answered at the station and she told him what she'd heard.

"Yep, he's here," Jaggerman's voice came though the cell. "Coach thought this was the safest place for him. I figured we'd hold him until everyone settles down. I'll turn him loose."

"No," Jess said. "Tempers are probably still a little raw. I'll bring his friends down to make sure he gets out safely."

"I don't think that's nec—"

"Better safe than sorry. Just hold him until we get there."

A pause. "Not sure I'm comfortable with that, Chief. Doesn't it violate his civil liberties or something?"

"No, we can hold him for up to twenty-four hours. I'll be there as soon as I can."

"Where are you? I thought I saw your Jeep over by the woods."

"You did. I got a report of a second body. It might be..." She trailed off. "I don't want to say too much. Just hold tight and let Wes know what's going on. I'll call if I find anything."

❧

WE TOOK JESS to see the grove with the pelts and tree markings first. She said she'd seen other trees with the markings elsewhere, and presumed they were Charlie's. The pelts, though, were new, and she had no idea what they meant.

We had a good idea where to find the body—I'd made note of the coordinates. As we approached, I noticed Clay slowing. Hesitating.

"Wrong turn?" I whispered as Jess trailed behind us.

"Thought I heard something. Wind's blowing the wrong way, though." He took another step, then lifted his hand, telling me to hold on while he investigated.

As he crept away, Jess moved up beside me. "Is that how they do things? Women and children in the rear?"

I didn't answer, partly because I was too busy watching Clay's back, partly because I just wasn't interested in defending myself. Our relationship wasn't perfect, but we've never had the caveman syndrome—where the big strong man insists on looking after his fragile little woman. With wolves, mated pairs are partners, equal partners, which only changes now, as we shift into our future roles.

There was a time when I would have felt the need to explain. To make sure she knew I wasn't "one of those women." I no longer cared. *I* knew I wasn't. Good enough.

Clay stopped beside a pine. After a moment, he waved me forward. When Jess tried to follow, he put up his hand to stop her.

"Like hell," she said. "I'm the one wearing a badge here and—"

I gave her a look. That's all it took. A look. Should I admit I was shocked when it actually worked? Maybe I was getting better at this Alpha thing. Or maybe that look just reminded her that I could rip that badge from her chest…and take her heart with it.

I crept over to Clay. He motioned for me to peer through the branches. When I did, I saw a figure in a parka heading for the body. A police parka.

"Kent," I whispered.

Jess had told Jaggerman to notify him. I should have said something then, warned her that we'd seen Kent taking way too much personal interest in the first corpse. Now it was obvious he wasn't just a creep with a camera. He was heading straight to the hidden body. Moving fast. Getting rid of the evidence.

I looked at Jess. She'd moved a few steps closer. I glanced toward Kent, then motioned for her to approach quietly. By the time she made it, Kent was crouching by the evergreen that sheltered the body. No time to explain. Well, yes, there was time, but I wasn't taking the chance that she'd blurt something and startle him. Instead, as she waited for an explanation, I motioned Clay around the other way. He took off.

I whispered, "Someone's there," and pointed to the spot where she could look through the branches. As she bent, I left her there and headed for Kent.

"I think you should let the chief handle that," I said as I walked up behind the crouched figure.

He jumped and turned and I saw his face. Not Kent. Jaggerman.

He looked at me, then to the left, where Clay blocked his escape.

"What the hell is going on here?" Jess said as she strode over. "Phil."

"I, uh, had a report. Must have been the same one you got."

"She got that from us," I said. "We were leading her here."

"Then someone else must have found the body too, I guess. I got a tip."

"Right after I said I was heading out here?" Jess said.

As Jaggerman continued backpedaling, it became very apparent why this career cop had been passed over for the chief's job. He was an idiot. There was no plausible way he could have "just happened" to beat us to the body, but he kept trying to find one.

I let Jess handle it while Clay and I blocked Jaggerman's exits. When he didn't even try to make a break for it, I started doing some logistical figuring.

"You weren't at the police station when Chief Dales called, were you," I said. "You were already out here. Which means you have the station phone forwarded to your cell."

"I...No, I got the call, then I—"

"Put on your jetpack to beat us here?" I took a step toward him. "Where's Morgan?"

He paused, then managed a weak, "Who?"

Clay was on Jaggerman so fast he didn't have time to squeak before he was up against a tree, suspended by his shirtfront.

"Hey!" Jess said. "That's my—"

"Where's Morgan?" Clay said.

"I don't know who—"

"The guy you supposedly took into custody."

"Oh, right. He's, um…I let him go." He looked at Jess. "I know you said not to, but I really felt I should. He was threatening lawsuits and—"

"You weren't at the station when she called," I said. "We've already established that. The only reason you were so damned determined to release Morgan was because you never had him in the first place, did you? Which means…" I looked at Jess. "Mrs. Rivera said Coach Hanlon took Morgan."

Coach Hanlon. Charlie's stepson.

I closed in on Jaggerman, pinned against the tree by Clay. "Where is Morgan?"

When he started to protest, Clay leaned in and whispered in his ear. I was standing too far back to hear more than a few words, but when Jaggerman's gaze shot to the tree sheltering the corpse, the message was clear. *Tell us or you'll end up like that.*

"Jess?" Jaggerman said in a strangled voice. "You know me. I've worked with you for years. I'm a good cop. I—"

"Tell him where his friend is," Jess said. "Or I need to start a search party for the guy, which means I'll have to ask *him* to escort you to the police station."

Jaggerman's jaw worked. Then he swallowed and said, "He's at the cave."

Silence. I checked my phone. The signal had disappeared. It came back at one bar for a second, then vanished again. I typed a text message repeating my request and sent it.

We'd been walking as I'd talked, and I'd kept my voice as low as I could. When I stopped speaking, though, we picked up voices. Faint ones, distant enough that we didn't need to worry about how much noise we made. We picked up our pace and strained to listen as we jogged toward them.

Then the voices went quiet. We slowed. A shot fired and we nearly dropped to the ground. Shouts followed. We froze, listening and straining to see.

Clay pointed and I picked up the faintest glimmer of a flashlight. Another shot sounded.

"There it is!" a man's voice bellowed. "I saw it. A wolf or a bear. Did you see it, boys?"

Something crashed through the woods. More voices. Excited now. Cries of, "I saw it!" and, "Over there!" They stayed at least a couple hundred feet away, so I knew it wasn't *us* they'd seen.

I looked at Clay.

"No idea, darling," he whispered.

I carefully stepped from behind the tree and peered around. I could see flashlights waving about and hear more crashing through the undergrowth. Then Morgan's scent slipped past on a breeze.

That snapped me back. It didn't matter *what* they were doing, only that they had Morgan. I held onto his scent as I started forward, Clay at my side. We moved from tree to tree, all the while listening to the shouts and cries. There were other noises, too, as we got closer. Snarls and grunts. Human, though; I could tell by the tenor.

I lost Morgan's scent once, but found it again and we began circling wide, staying away from the noise. Gradually, as we got closer, the two separated, the cacophony to my left, Morgan's scent to my right. They weren't far apart, just enough for us to creep in Morgan's direction.

Finally, I knew where he was. In a cluster of trees. Staying in place, if his scent was right. I started motioning for Clay to go around, then stopped and told him to stay where he was. I'd circle. The noise was far to our left, so he didn't argue.

I rounded the cluster of trees. I got just north of it when I heard the soft thump of feet running through the snow. I turned to see Morgan racing toward me. He was holding his hands in front of him and there was something pale against his mouth. Before I could say a word, he lunged and slammed into me. We both went down.

By the time Clay came running, I was sitting on the ground, pulling at the cord binding Morgan's hands. It wasn't easy. He kept struggling, his voice muffled against the gag. Clay grabbed him by the collar and I got his hands free.

Morgan ripped off the duct tape over his mouth, hissing at the pain, then whispering, "Down!" to Clay, then to me, "Get down!"

As I motioned for us to move to the cluster of trees, dry branches crackled and snow crunched. A figure lurched into view. It was a teenage boy, staggering and stumbling. I shot to my feet.

"No!" Morgan said, but I was already running toward the boy.

He stopped and stared at me with unfocused eyes.

"It's okay," I whispered as I got close. "We're—"

With a snarl, he swung something. I saw it coming and ducked just in time. It hit my shoulder, the blow barely penetrating my jacket. The boy pounced. He hit me full on. I staggered back and I would have been fine if I hadn't slipped on something—a rock or a log—and lost my balance. I went down with him on top of me.

The boy snarled and tried to pin me by the shoulders. I saw a flash of teeth as his open mouth shot for my neck.

He's trying to bite me.

I grabbed the boy and held him off. Then Clay was behind him, hands on his jacket, whipping him up in the air. As the boy hung there, he gnashed his teeth and spat and snarled like a wild beast. He swung something again. A club, I realized as I snatched it from him. A police baton.

Morgan slapped his duct tape over the kid's mouth. The boy continued to struggle and growl.

"I think we know where those hallucinogens went," Clay muttered.

"They're drugged," Morgan said. "They gave me something, too. A sedative, I think. Same as I had the first night I got here."

"Are you okay?"

"Woozy. They underestimated the dose." It took a lot to knock out a werewolf. "And I know what it is this time, so I can fight it."

Holding the struggling boy, Clay looked toward the noises on our left. "How many are there?"

"Minus this one? The coach and four players."

"Players?" I said. "Football?"

"It's some kind of—"

At a noise to our left, Morgan stopped and we all looked over. Everything had gone quiet. I tried to pick up a scent, but the wind was blowing the wrong way. A twig cracked. Then snow squeaked underfoot. I pointed in the direction of the sounds.

"Circling us," Clay said.

I took hold of the boy and sent Clay to investigate. Morgan followed. I glanced at the kid. Just a regular teenage boy. My height. Muscular. Wearing a team jacket.

A football player, Morgan had said. Why would the coach be drugging—?

A shot fired. Clay grabbed Morgan and knocked him down. I did the same with the boy. When he kept struggling, I dragged him over and tied his hands with the cord they'd used on Morgan. I peered over at Morgan and Clay. They were still on the ground, crawling backward toward us.

"One shooter," Clay murmured when he was close enough. "Over there." He pointed to where he'd been heading.

"It's the coach," Morgan whispered. "The kids have clubs. The coach has a rifle. He was shooting at me to get me to run."

"Hunting you?" I said.

He nodded. I'd seen something like that before, years ago, a guy who'd captured and hunted supernaturals.

"Does he know what you are?" I whispered.

Morgan shook his head. "I don't think so. He kept talking about wolves and bears and predators, but he didn't seem to get the connection."

"Any sign of magic?"

"It's definitely some sort of ritual. That's what they were doing in the cave. The coach brought the kids there. He kept me outside, so they couldn't see me, but I could hear enough to figure out what was going on. He gave them something to drink. It sounded like they'd done it before—no one asked what was going on. Then he started leading them in some kind of vision quest. All this mumbo-jumbo about how they were mighty hunters and—"

My phone vibrated. It didn't ring, but the vibration sounded so loud that I hit Ignore.

"The police chief?" Morgan said, leaning over.

I nodded. "I'm going to text her the coordinates and—"

A shot whizzed past.

"Boys!" a voice yelled. "Over here. I've got it cornered."

It. Why did they keep saying…? Didn't matter, as Clay would say. I started to prairie-dog-pop from the bushes, but he pushed me down and did it for me. He pointed and mouthed, "Hundred feet."

Damn, Hanlon was close. Unlike the kids, he was obviously good at sneaking through the forest. Our whispers must have been carrying more than we thought. Judging by that shot, he knew exactly where we were.

I signaled a plan. Morgan was to stay where he was—he might protest that he felt fine, but he'd been drugged. Clay and I set out.

I went north, Clay south. Hanlon kept shouting for the boys, which made him very easy to track. He wasn't moving anyway. Just standing there, yelling. We crept in until we could see each other on either side of Hanlon. Then Clay charged.

As Clay took Hanlon down, I heard Morgan shout. Then I caught the snarl and snap and pound of a running pack. Clay pinned Hanlon as Morgan raced over.

"They're—" he started.

The boys appeared. Four of them, running together, howling, waving their batons.

"Get it, boys!" Hanlon shouted. "It's the bear. Get it!"

The first one charged Morgan. I caught a whiff of the boy's scent and recognized him as the vandal who'd slashed our tires and broken into our rooms. Morgan tried to swing around to face him, but he was feeling the effects of that sedative and stumbled. I swooped in and grabbed the kid by the arm. I threw him back with the others.

"It's a pack," Hanlon yelled. "You stumbled into a pack of bears. Kill them! Before they attack!"

The boys rushed us. I kicked one away. Morgan body-slammed another.

"We're not bears," I said. "We're people. *Look* harder. *Listen*."

The sound of my voice made them hesitate. That's why Hanlon gagged Morgan—so nothing would disrupt the illusion. They hung there, clutching their cudgels, eyes struggling to focus.

"You've been drugged," I said. "You're confused. But we're talking. That means we're people. Just like you."

"No!" Hanlon yelled. "They're monsters. That's what we've been hunting. I thought it was bears, but it's monsters.

Look over there." He pointed at the fifth boy, the one we'd bound and gagged, stumbling toward them. "It's Bryan. They caught him and they were going to kill him, just like they killed Ricky. You remember what happened to Ricky? The bear got him. We were hunting and it—"

Clay slammed Hanlon's face into the snow.

"Thank you," I said. "Now, boys, you're confused. You know you are. But we're here to help. You're from Westwood, New York. You're on the football—"

A hiss of pain behind me. I turned to see Hanlon with a knife. He must have pulled it from his pocket. He'd surprised Clay by slashing at him. Clay let go just long enough for Hanlon to rise. Clay grabbed the back of his jacket, but Hanlon was wrenching down the zipper as I raced over.

Hanlon got free of his jacket and started to run. We went after him. The boys went after him, too. They barreled past me, shoving me aside. I thought they were running with him. Then I saw their faces and heard their snarls and realized what they saw—running prey.

They pounced on their coach, beating and biting as he fought and screamed.

Nineteen

"SO IT WASN'T an actual ritual," Morgan said as we sat at the police station. "Just a mishmash?"

"It's not an uncommon belief," Clay said. "Imbibing the strength of your enemy."

"By literally imbibing them?" Morgan shook his head. "I hope those kids never find out what they did."

"They won't if their parents can help it," I said.

"What a mess," Morgan said, shaking his head. "A crazy, fucked-up mess."

It was indeed a mess, one that Jessica Dales and the town of Westwood would be digging out from for a long time. Jessica had kept us informed as she questioned Hanlon and Jaggerman, and we'd pieced together what we could. It had started with Charlie Lacoste. Like most academics—professional or not—he'd focused his attention on one specific area of interest. For him, it was rituals of consumption and transfer, whether it was drinking bear blood or eating your enemies in an attempt to appropriate their strength. It was, as Jess had said, strictly academic. That's where the fight with his stepson began, when Charlie's wife got sick and Tom Hanlon somehow got it into his head that one of his stepfather's rituals might help—if not to save his mother, then at least to give her the strength to undergo treatment.

Town legend said that after his wife's death, Charlie went off the rails, but it seemed more that his son drove him there. Hanlon had done his own research when Charlie refused to help, and after his mother's death, he became obsessed with what he'd learned. He came up with a new application for his obsession—using these rituals to help his football team win.

Yes, football. It didn't seem any less crazy now than it had when we first discovered the connection. Even after talking to Hanlon, it didn't make more sense. Somehow, it had to Jaggerman, though, the volunteer assistant coach who'd been his wingman in all this. It had also apparently made sense to Hanlon's girlfriend, Marnie, the server at the diner, who'd canceled our repair service. She was also the one who'd drugged Morgan the other night at the diner and called Hanlon to say she'd found a victim.

That's who they targeted—drifters. Young men, strong and healthy. They set them loose in the forests with the key members of the football team, who'd been drugged and brainwashed into thinking they were still in the cave, imagining a vision where they were seeing animals, which they'd hunt and then, yes, partially eat, to imbibe their strength.

It had even seemed to work, taking a losing team to the state finals for the past three years running. I'd say it was the power of suggestion. When these boys came out of their drug-induced state, they knew only that they'd undergone a powerful magical ritual that made them better players. They believed it; they won. In those three years, four graduating team players got a full college ride, several more got partial scholarships. I think it was hard for me to really comprehend the importance of that for a town like Westwood. For many of these kids, college had never been an option. Now it was.

There was the matter of town pride, too. I think I couldn't quite understand the importance of that either. But I could see it, in the signs and the murals. They had a winning team; their children were winners; their town was a winner. That's what drew Jaggerman and Hanlon's girlfriend into his mad scheme.

It *was* mad, of course. Tom Hanlon was not a sane man. No one could be, to hatch such a plot. He'd almost certainly murdered his stepfather. From what we could tell, Charlie finally figured out what his stepson was doing. That's when he vanished.

And Ricky Rivera? That might be the biggest tragedy of all. Hanlon implied he'd been killed by one of their victims.

Maybe he had, but Hanlon said a few things later that made Jessica suspect Ricky's own teammates had done it. Ricky had been weak, Hanlon had ranted. They'd tried to include him, but the others "smelled weakness." I don't know if that's true. I only know that if it is, I hope to God those boys never remember it. And I hoped to God the Riveras never learned the truth. The death of their son would be enough for them.

"ARE YOU GOING to be okay?" I asked Jessica.

We were in her office, Clay and I, Morgan outside with Kent, who seemed shell-shocked and really wasn't much help. There was no sign he'd played any role in what happened. If he had, I'm sure Jaggerman would have dragged him down with him. So why had he been taking photos? I wasn't asking and I wasn't telling Jessica. I'd have to at some point—she needed to know that he could be a problem—but she had enough to deal with.

She hadn't answered my question, just sat there, drinking hot chocolate, staring into space. I asked again.

"I don't know," she said. "This is beyond...I've seen things. I've heard things. You know what it's like in our world. But this...I don't understand. I really do not understand."

"I don't think it helps to try," I said. "The state police or the FBI or someone will come in and take over and you just have to step back and let them. Protect your town. Protect the kids. They didn't do anything wrong."

"I know." She exhaled. "I have to question Jason, though. The boy who vandalized your vehicles. He searched your rooms, too—he works at the motel sometimes. He was one of the boys out there."

"I saw him."

She swallowed. "I'm hoping Hanlon just made up a story to get Jason to slash your tires and search your rooms, but…I don't know. Wouldn't he have thought it was odd if one of you guys suddenly went missing?"

"Maybe, maybe not. Hanlon seemed to have a real hold over the boys. He probably just fed him a really good story. Told him we were…I don't know, spies from a rival team? Faked Morgan's disappearance to upset the town and throw the team's game?"

"Football." She shook her head. "All this for football."

It was more than football, but as I'd said, it didn't help to tease out all of the motivations. Ultimately, what Hanlon, Jaggerman and Marnie did would still be incomprehensible. "Question Jason. Question Hanlon *about* Jason. If the kid seems clean, keep a really good eye on him for a while. Just in case."

She nodded. "I will."

WE LEFT JESSICA to her work, with an invitation to call me if she needed to talk about anything on the case. Or if she had concerns about having the Pack living so close to her town. I gave her Paige's contact information, too, in case she wanted support from that angle.

Both cars had been repaired. We drove Morgan to his.

"Can I follow you guys to Stonehaven?" he said. "Or would you rather take a breather at home and I'll come by in a day or two?"

I twisted to look at him. "I thought you were leaving."

"I was. Then I changed my mind and came back, which is how I saw that kid and nearly got myself killed." He paused. "On second thought, maybe that's a sign."

"Only that you should have joined us for breakfast instead of taking off. You should come for the weekend. The Sorrentinos are driving up tonight with the boys. It's not an official Meet, but a good way to observe the Pack in its natural habitat. As long as you don't mind the noise. Seven werewolves and two five-year-olds means a very chaotic household."

"As long as no one tries to kidnap or hunt me, I'm fine."

"Actually..." I glanced at Clay. "We can't guarantee that. But we will ask them to go easy on you."

"All right then. You have an extra houseguest."

I smiled. "Good. You can follow us back."

❧

WE CALLED JEREMY to tell him we were bringing Morgan. When we arrived, Morgan asked to head out back first, get a look at the property. Giving us time to say hi to the kids. I appreciated that, especially considering that our children seemed to have inherited some of Clay's "no strangers in my den" attitude. I'm sure Jeremy had warned them, but they'd be more comfortable meeting Morgan outside and bringing him in after introductions.

Clay and I walked into the house and braced for shouts and pounding feet.

"We're home!" I called.

Silence.

"Hey!" Clay bellowed. "Anyone here?"

When no one answered, my heart started tripping. Ridiculous, I know. It's a big house. They could be in the back room, watching videos, or upstairs, Kate plugged into her iPod, Logan engrossed in a book.

I yelled again. Still nothing. I checked the garage. My car was there. So was Clay's.

I took a deep breath and went for the back door, moving fast. Clay didn't tell me I was being foolish—that Jeremy was with them, that this was our house, that nothing could have possibly happened. He knew it didn't matter. All I could think about was what had happened in Westwood. About the families of those young men who'd passed through, lost young men, their families waiting, hoping for a call, dreading a call.

Most of all, though, I thought of Ricky Rivera, the smiling boy in the photo, the horror of his death. I thought of his mother's rage, his father's quiet grief. I thought of that sign on their lawn. And I thought of that light. That single light, burning for the child who'd never come home.

The back door was locked. As I fumbled with it, Clay reached over and pulled it open, then stuck his head out, shouting so loud it made my ears ring. I stepped outside. Morgan was in the yard. He turned to us, looking confused.

"Do you see—?" I began.

"Mommy!" a voice shouted behind me.

I turned as Kate thumped down the hall, dragging her foot. She launched herself and sent me smacking into the wall as I caught her.

"We were hiding," Logan said as he walked toward us. "You were supposed to come find us."

Of course. An old trick, one I should have guessed. In trying to take charge of the investigation, I hadn't shared much with Jeremy, certainly not enough for him to have any clue that I'd panic when the kids didn't come running.

When I didn't reply, Kate pulled back. "What's wrong, Mommy?"

I hugged her, as tight as I could. "Nothing," I whispered. "Nothing at all."

It *was* nothing. No reason to worry any more than I already did, which was probably enough for a half-dozen anxious parents.

No one was going to break into Stonehaven and steal our children. No one was going to sneak onto the playground and steal them there either. I looked at Kate's foot, and while I still felt a pang of guilt, I knew I'd been overreacting yesterday to think she could have been snatched during my brief moment of inattention. I'd heard her scream. I'd been there in seconds.

We had to be vigilant. There was no question of that. While the chance of a stranger grabbing our children was slight, the chance of a mutt trying it was much higher, and it would only grow as our children did, moving farther from the safety of the den.

We couldn't be with them all the time. But we could train them to look out for themselves. We'd already taken the first step last year, letting them know what we were. The door was open, not to frighten them, but to warn them, to make them aware of what it meant to be the children of the Pack.

I boosted Kate up onto my hip. "So I hear we're having company this weekend."

"Uncle Nick and Uncle Antonio and Reese and Noah."

"Maybe even Karl and Hope," Logan said. "Hope was talking to Jeremy and she said they have news. Special news. They might come up and tell all of us."

I glanced at Jeremy, now beside Clay. He nodded, "Special news."

"Well, that does sound intriguing. We'll have another guest here, too. Someone I'd like you to meet. Let's head out and say hi."

With Kate on my hip, I took Logan's hand, smiled at Clay and Jeremy, and led the kids to meet Morgan.